BACKFLASH

BACKFLASH

Richard Stark

CHIVERS

British Library Cataloguing in Publication Data available

This Large Print edition published by AudioGO Ltd, Bath, 2013.
Published by arrangement with Quercus Editions Ltd (UK)

U.K. Hardcover   ISBN   978 1 4713 4256 1
U.K. Softcover   ISBN   978 1 4713 4257 8

Printed and bound in Great Britain by TJ International Limited

*This is for Walter and Carol,
who got married tomorrow.*

ONE

1

When the car stopped rolling, Parker kicked out the rest of the windshield and crawled through on to the wrinkled hood, Glock first. He slid to the left, around the tree that had made the Seville finally jolt to a stop, and listened. The siren receded, far upslope. These woods held a shocked silence, after the crash; every animal ear in a hundred yards was as alert as Parker's.

Nobody came down the hill, following the scar through the trees. There was just the one car in pursuit up there, federal agents of some kind, probably trying right now to make radio contact with the rest of their crew, and still chasing the truck with the rockets, figuring they'd come back to the wrecked car later.

Later was good enough for Parker. He eased around the tree and bent to move down the less-battered right side of the Seville, where he'd been seated next to the driver. The glass from that window was gone; he looked in at Howell at the wheel, and Howell looked back, his eyes scared, but his mouth twisted in what was supposed to be an ironic grin. 'They clamped me,' he said, and shook his head.

Parker looked at him. The firewall and steering column and door had all folded in on him, like he was the jelly in the doughnut. He'd live, but it would take two acetylene torches four hours to cut him out of there. 'You're fucked,' Parker told him.

'I thought I was,' Howell said.

Parker moved on and tried to open the rear door, which still had its glass, but it was jammed. He smashed out the window with the barrel of the Clock, reached in, grabbed the workout bag by the handle, and pulled it out through the new hole. Bag in left hand, Glock in right, he moved over again to look in at Howell, and Howell hadn't moved. He was still looking out, at Parker. Howell was mostly bald, and his head was streaked with bleeding cuts and hobnailed with hard drops of sweat. He breathed through his open mouth, and kept looking at Parker. His legs and torso and left: arm were clamped, but his right arm was free. His pistol was on the seat by his right hip. He could reach it, but he left it there, and looked at Parker, and breathed through his open mouth, and more blood and more sweat oozed out on to his bald head.

Parker hefted the bag, and the Glock. Howell shook his head. 'Come on, Parker,' he said. 'You know me better than that.'

Parker considered him. He didn't like to leave a loose end behind, sometimes they followed you, they showed up later when you

2

were trying to think about something else. He moved the Glock slightly, rested the barrel on the open window.

Howell said, 'You know me, Parker.'

'And you know me.'

'Not anymore.' Howell smiled, showing bloodlined teeth, and said, 'This crash knocked my memory loose. I don't even know who *I* am, anymore. It's all gone.'

'They'll try to make it worth your while, bargain you down.'

'Not worth my while,' Howell said. 'Not with you out there. I'll catch up on my reading.'

Parker thought about it. He knew Howell, he trusted him on the job, they'd watch each other's back, they'd give each other a straight count when the jackpot was in. But for the long haul?

Howell nodded at the bag. 'Have a beer on me,' he suggested.

Parker nodded, and made up his mind. 'See you in twenty years,' he said, and turned away, to head downslope.

'I'll be rested,' Howell called after him.

2

It was a house on a lake called Colliver Pond, seventy miles from New York, a deep rural corner where New York and New Jersey and

3

Pennsylvania meet. A narrow blacktop road skirted the lake, among the pines, and the house, gray stone and brown shingle, squatted quiet and inconspicuous between road and shore. Now, in April, the trees not yet fully leafed out, the clapboard houses on both sides could clearly be seen, each of them less than fifty feet away, but it didn't matter; they were empty. This was mostly a resort community, lower-level white-collar, people who came here three months every summer and left their 'cottages' unoccupied the rest of the year. Only fifteen per cent of the houses around the lake were lived in full-time, and most of those were over on the other side, in the lee of the mountain, out of the winter wind.

For Parker, it was ideal. A place to stay, to lie low when nothing was going on, a 'home' as people called it, and no neighbors. In the summer, when the clerks came out to swim and fish and boat, Parker and Claire went somewhere else.

Late afternoon, amber lights warm in the windows. Parker turned in at the driveway, at the wheel of a red Subaru, two days and three cars since the Seville had gone off that mountain road and he'd left Howell behind. The Subaru was a mace, a safe car, not in any cop's computer, so long as nobody looked too closely at the paperwork and the serial numbers. Parker steered it down the drive through the trees and shrubbery that took the

4

place of the lawn here, and ahead of him the left side door of the double attached garage slid upward; so Claire had seen him coming. He drove in and got out of the car as the door slid down, and Claire was in the yellow-lit rectangle of doorway to the kitchen. 'Welcome home, Mr Lynch,' she said.

Claire had jokes, and that was one of them; they were all wasted on Parker. She'd known him as Lynch when they'd first met, so she liked to greet him with that name, because it showed they had a history. She wanted to believe they had a history, in both directions.

'Hello,' he said, and crossed out of the garage, carrying the workout bag. He stopped in the doorway to kiss her, and in that move opened himself again to all the warmth he'd shut out since he'd gone away. The homecomings were always good, because they were a kind of coming back to life.

After the kiss, she smiled at him and took his hand and nodded at the workout bag: 'Not the laundry,' she suggested.

'A hundred forty thousand,' he told her. 'Supposed to be. I didn't count it yet.'

'I like it that you save the fun parts for me,' she said.

What she meant was, she didn't want any part of it at all, what happened when he was away. They'd met in the first place because her ex-brother-in-law, an idiot named Billy Lebatard, had involved her in a robbery at a coin convention that had gone very sour. At the end of it, Billy was dead, there was blood everywhere, and Parker had dragged Claire into safety at the last second. She'd been married once, earlier, to an airline pilot who'd died in a crash; with that, and the mess Billy'd made, she wanted no more. Once, a couple of hard-edged clowns had broken in here, but Parker had dealt with it, and now he and Claire were together most of the time, warming themselves at each other's fire, liking the calm. When Parker went away, as he sometimes did, she wanted to know nothing about it. She was willing, at the most, while he showered, to count the money and leave it in stacks on the coffee table in the living room for him to see when he came in, wearing a black robe and carrying a glass. She sat on the sofa without expression and said, 'A hundred forty thousand exactly.'

'Good.'

'Just like the paper said.'

He sat on the sofa beside her and cocked his head. 'The paper?'

'You haven't read any newspapers?'

'I've been moving.'

'Before you went away,' she said, 'a man named Howell phoned you.'

'Right.'

'A man named Howell is dead.'

That surprised him. 'Dead? How dead?'

'Injuries from an automobile accident.

6

While escaping, the car he drove crashed down a mountainside. The other three people, and a small truck with anti-tank rockets, all escaped. Arrests are expected.'

'They killed him,' Parker said.

'Who killed him?'

'The law. Feds or local. Let me see the paper.'

She got up and crossed to the refectory table near the stone fireplace, and brought back a day-old paper turned to the national news page. Handing it to him, sitting again beside him, she said, 'Would they kill him?'

'They were in a hurry,' Parker told her. 'They wanted names, they wanted to know where we'd be. Especially because they lost the rockets. Howell was hurt, but he wouldn't tell them anything. We talked about it before I left, and he said he wouldn't tell them anything, and I believed him, and it turns out I was right. And they were in such a hurry, they didn't wait to see how much he was wounded, maybe hurt inside, before they leaned on him, and he died.'

'Poor Mr Howell,' she said.

'He wasn't really much of a reader anyway,' Parker said, and turned to the newspaper, which told him several things he knew and nothing he didn't. Three rogue Marines had been trading with a terrorist group, selling them weapons stolen from a military depot. There was to be an exchange, rockets for cash. The two groups didn't know there were two other groups involved as well; the Feds, who'd got wind of the thefts at the depot and were trying to follow the trail, and the four professional thieves who showed up at the transfer point meaning to take everything from everybody. Which they did, at the cost of one of their own, a man named Marshall Howell. The Feds expected to round up the other three momentarily.

Parker put the paper down and said, 'That's the end of it. The other two keep the rockets, sell them to somebody else. I keep this.' And he nodded at the money.

Claire pointed at the newspaper. 'That could have been you.'

'It always could,' he said. 'So far, it isn't. I go away, and I come back.'

She looked at him. 'Every time?'

'Except the last time,' he said.

She put her arms around him, touched her lips to the spot where the pulse beat in his throat. 'Later,' she said, 'let's have a fire.'

3

The best place to hide money is in somebody else's house. The morning after he got back, Parker filled seven Ziploc bags with ten thousand dollars each, put them in the pockets of his windbreaker, and went for a walk along the lakefront.

There were five houses along here he'd previously set up for himself, both as drops and as potential backup sites if trouble ever came too close. He'd made simple clean access to each house and prepared banks for himself in all of them. A false joist in a crawlspace; an extra ceiling in a closet; a new pocket in the wall behind a kitchen drawer. These people all liked their summer houses just the way they were, but it would pay them, though they didn't know it, to remodel.

He was gone not quite an hour, a householder taking a long casual walk along the lake in the thin spring sunlight, and when he got back to the house Claire said, 'Mr Howell called.'

Parker looked at her, and waited.

She smiled slightly. 'Mr Marshall Howell.'

'Did he?'

'He left a number where you could call him.'

He made a bark of laughter. 'That must be some number,' he said, and took off the windbreaker and read the phone number on the pad in the kitchen, then opened the phone book to see where that area code was. 518. Upstate New York, around Albany.

He used the kitchen phone to make the call, and after four rings a recorded woman's voice, sounding like somebody's secretary, announced the number he'd just dialed, then crisply said, 'Please leave a name and number after the tone. Thank you.'

No. Parker waited for the tone, then said, 'Mr Howell will phone at three o'clock,' and hung up, and at three o'clock he stepped into the phone booth at the Mobil station out on the highway to New York, the only enclosed phone booth within eight miles, and dialed the number again.

One ring, and the man who answered sounded fat, middle-aged, wheezy. 'Cathman,' he said.

'Not Mr Howell,' Parker said.

A wheezy chuckle. 'Not really possible,' Cathman said. 'That's Mr Parker, isn't it?'

'I don't know anybody named Cathman,' Parker said.

'We're meeting now, in a way,' Cathman pointed out. 'The fact is, Mr Howell was going to be doing something for me, but he told me he had this other project with you first, and then we could get together to plan our own enterprise. Unfortunately, he didn't survive that earlier obligation.'

Parker waited. Was he supposed to be responsible for this fellow's plans coming apart?

Cathman said, 'I don't want to sound forward, Mr Parker, but I believe you share much of the expertise I found so valuable in Mr Howell.'

'Possibly.' If this was an entrapment call, it

10

was the flakiest on record.

'I expect,' Cathman said, 'you're not particularly looking for work at the moment, since I believe your part of the activity just completed was rather more successful than our friend Howell's.'

'Oh,' Parker said. 'You want me to take Howell's place.'

'If,' Cathman said. 'If you're interested in further work in, well, not the same line. A similar line. If you'd prefer to rest, take time off, of course I'll understand. In that case, if you could recommend someone . . .'

This fellow, whoever he was, was recruiting people for some sort of criminal undertaking *over the telephone.* Had Howell really taken this clown seriously? Or had Howell been interested in something else, that Cathman didn't realize? Parker said, 'I don't make recommendations.

'But would you be— Well, would you care to meet? There are things, you understand, one doesn't say on the phone.'

Well, he knew that much, though he didn't seem to understand the concept in its entirety. Parker said, 'A meet. For you to tell me what Howell was going to do for you.'

'Just so. You could come here, or if you prefer I could go to you. I'm not exactly sure where you are . . .'

Good. Parker said, 'Howell gave you this phone number?'

'His wife did. I presume she's his wife.'

'I'll come to you,' Parker decided, because Cathman sounded more dangerous than interesting. He had no sense of self-preservation, and he was walking around with knowledge that could hurt other people. If he turned out to have something interesting, Parker might go along with it, take Howell's place. If not, Parker might switch him off before his broadcasting interfered with anybody serious.

'Oh, fine,' Cathman said. 'We could do lunch, if you—'

'A meet,' Parker said. 'Your territory. Outside. A parking lot, a farmer's market, a city park.'

'Oh, I know,' Cathman said. 'The perfect place. Amtrak comes up the Hudson. Could you take the train, from Penn Station? In New York.'

'Yes.'

'It's less than two hours up, the stop is called Rhinecliff. Wait, I have the schedule here. What would be a good day?'

'Tomorrow.'

'That's wonderful. All right, let me see. Yes, you take the train at three-fifty tomorrow afternoon, you'll get to Rhinecliff at five twenty-eight. I'll come down from Albany, my train gets there at four fifty-one, so I'll just wait on the platform. You'll find me, I'm heavyset, and I have about as much hair as our

12

poor friend Howell, and I'll be wearing a gray topcoat. Oh, and probably a gray hat as well, so the baldness doesn't help, does it?'

'I'll find you,' Parker said.

4

Amtrak was new, but the station at Rhinecliff was old, one end of it no longer in use, rusted remains of steel walkways and stairs looming upward against the sky like the ruins of an earlier civilization, which is what they were. At the still-working end of the platform, a long metal staircase climbed to a high enclosed structure that led above the tracks over to the old station building. The land here was steep, coming up from the river, leveling for the tracks, then continuing sharply upward.

A dozen people got off the train with Parker, and another two or three got on. He came down to the concrete last, the only passenger without luggage, and stood on the platform while the rest of them trudged up the stairs and the train jerked forward behind him. In his dark windbreaker and black chinos and heavy black shoes, he looked like some sort of skilled workman, freelancing, brought in by a contractor to do one specific job. Which he was.

The stairs were to his right, with the people

slowly receding upward. Along the platform were three or four backless benches, and on one of them, down to the left, sat a dumpy man in a pearl-gray topcoat and hat, his back to the train now leaving as he gazed out and down at the river.

When the train was gone, Parker turned to look across the track at a chain-link fence, and a parking lot, and a steep hillside, and a curving steep street, and some old houses. One passenger, having climbed up this set of stairs, was now thudding down a second staircase over there, headed for the parking lot. He was rumpled, in his forties, wearing an anorak that was too heavy for this season, and carrying a thick heavy briefcase. He seemed to be muttering to himself.

Parker watched that fellow descend, and the man never looked in this direction. At the foot of the stairs, he turned and hurried along between the rows of cars, fishing his keys out of his pocket as he went. He hit his electronic opener and a Saab over there went *beep* and flashed its amber lights. The man reached his car, tossed the briefcase in the back, got behind the wheel, and drove out of there. In the car, his lips were still moving. He didn't show interest in anything at all outside his own head. So there must be a college around here somewhere.

The Saab drove up the steep street and made the turn, and went out of sight. Then

14

Parker walked along the platform to Cathman, who looked up and smiled and nodded. 'Good afternoon,' he said.

The bench was long enough so they could both be on it with some space between. Parker sat next to Cathman and said, 'You aren't in the same business as Howell.'

Cathman laughed, self-conscious. 'Heavens, no. Not at all. That's why I *needed* Mr Howell. Or you. Or whoever it might be.'

'You just go around talking to people? In bars, and here and there?'

'Certainly not,' Cathman said, and gave Parker a sudden keen look. He said, 'Mr Parker, I don't know your world very well, or your . . . business. But that doesn't mean I'm a fool.'

'Uh huh.'

'I am not going to talk to an undercover policeman, believe me.'

'Maybe you are right now,' Parker told him.

Cathman smirked, and shook his head. 'I was sure of Mr Howell,' he said, 'and I'm sure of you. Mr Parker, do you gamble?'

'Not with people I don't know.'

Cathman made a sudden irritated hand-gesture, sweeping away a misunderstanding. 'I don't mean that,' he said. 'I mean gambling, legal gambling. Lotteries, betting parlors. Las Vegas, Atlantic City, Foxwood.'

Parker looked at him: 'Foxwood?'·

Cathman's hand-wave this time was airy,

dismissive. 'Over in Connecticut,' he said. 'On the Indian reservation, so state laws don't apply. The casino there makes millions.'

Parker nodded. 'So the Indians finally found a way to beat the white man.'

'My question was, do you gamble?'

'No.'

'May I ask why not?'

What did this have to do with anything? But Parker had learned, over the years, that when somebody wants to tell you his story, you have to let him tell it his own way. Try to push him along, speed it up, you'll just confuse him and slow him down.

So the question is, why not gamble? Parker'd never thought about it, he just knew it was pointless and uninteresting. He said, 'Turn myself over to random events? Why? The point is to try to control events, and they'll still get away from you anyway. Why make things worse? Jump out a window, see if a mattress truck goes by. Why? Only if the room's on fire.'

That was apparently the right answer. Cathman beamed like a man who'd won the turkey at the raffle. He said, 'The reason you feel that way, Mr Parker, if I may presume, and the reason *I* feel that way, is, we are not in despair. We are not bored and miserable with our own lives. We don't pay twenty dollars every week for a cluster of numbers in the state lottery, in hopes we're buying a new

16

car, a new house, a new job, a new wife, better children and a firmer stomach. Gambling preys on misery, Mr Parker, misery and discontent. Where the people are comfortable and confident, gambling does not flourish.'

Parker was beginning to see that Cathman was not a man with a job, he was a man with a cause. So why did he need a Howell, or a Parker? He said, 'Tell me where you're going with this.'

'Let me first tell you who I am,' Cathman said, and reached inside his topcoat. Parker tensed, looking at the Adam's apple he'd hit, but what Cathman brought out was a small flat leather case. Opening it, he took out a business card and handed it over. Parker took it:

HILLIARD CATHMAN

Hilliard Cathman Associates
Urban & Policy Planning
Resource Apportionment Consultants

14-162 State Plaza
Suite 1100
Albany, NY 12961

518 828-3344   fax 518 828-3388

'Since I retired from state government,' Cathman explained, 'I've been able to use my contacts and expertise in a broader and more satisfying way. Not limited to New York State any more, nor to one administration.'

Parker extended the card, but Cathman waved it away: 'No, keep it. I want you to understand. I am knowledgeable, and I am reliable. In my area. As Mr Howell was in his, and as he led me to believe you are in yours.'

'I still don't see where we're going,' Parker said.

Cathman looked out at the river, apparently to gather his thoughts. The river was wide here, and moved briskly. It was a hundred miles from here to the harbor and the sea.

Cathman said, 'Gambling fever has struck the politicians, I'm afraid. They see it as a safe form of taxation, a way to collect money from the people without causing discontent or taxpayer revolt. The lottery does it, and OTB does it, and casino gambling can do it. Three resort areas in New York State have been designated by the state legislature for legalized gambling. This area is not one of them.'

'Then they're lucky,' Parker said.

'Yes, they are, but they don't know it. Foxwood in particular has driven them wild. It's so close, and it's so profitable. So a new bill has worked its way through the legislature, and will be signed before the end of the month, which adds a fourth gambling district in New

18

York State.' He gestured outward: 'The river.'

'A casino boat?'

'Yes. There are any number of them around America, and they tend to be migratory, as laws change, state by state. The boat which will be used on the Hudson, between Poughkeepsie and Albany, which is at this moment steaming up the Atlantic coast toward its new assignment, was until recently called the *Spirit of Biloxi*. But there are so many casinos in the Biloxi area now, the competition is so fierce, that the owners of the boat had no problem with the idea of changing its name to the *Spirit of the Hudson*.'

'Loyalty,' suggested Parker.

'They have nailed their colors to a weathervane,' Cathman agreed. 'At this point,' he went on, 'because there is a strong anti-gambling faction in the legislature—or, that is, several anti-gambling factions, some religious, some practical, some spiteful—approval has been given only for a four-month trial period. And, since they have learned from OTB and elsewhere that people will, if given the chance, spend far beyond their income when the gambling bug strikes, for this four-month trial period only, no credit will be allowed.'

Parker frowned. 'They can't do it. It doesn't work that way.'

'Nevertheless, that is the compromise that has been struck. If the four-month trial is considered a success, and the boat continues

19

to be the *Spirit of the Hudson*, then credit wagering will be permitted. But during the trial period, no. No credit cards, no checks, no letters of credit.'

'Cash,' Parker said.

Cathman nodded. 'A boat swimming in cash,' he said. 'Through my access to various government departments, I can obtain virtually any information you could possibly need. Blueprints of the boat, details of security, employee backgrounds, locations of safes, schedules, security arrangements at the two ports where the ship will touch land, being Albany and Poughkeepsie, the turnaround points. The details of any robbery that might take place on the boat, of course, are your concern.'

'And what do you want for this?'

Cathman shrugged inside his expensive topcoat. 'I'm a little tired,' he said. 'I would like to live in a state with less severe winters, pick and choose my clients with more freedom. If you proceed, and if you are successful, I would like ten per cent.'

'You're gambling,' Parker told him.

Cathman's smile was wan. 'I hope not,' he said. 'If I am dealing with professionals, and I know myself to be professional in my own line of work, is that gambling? I don't think so. You'll have no reason to begrudge me my ten per cent.'

'You're the inside man,' Parker pointed out.

20

'The law will be looking for the inside man.'

Now Cathman laughed outright. 'Me? Mr Parker, no one in New York State government would suspect me of so much as taking paper clips home from the office. My reputation is so clear, and for so long, that no one would think of me as the inside man for a second. And there would be dozens of others who might have been the ones who helped with inside information.'

Parker nodded. He thought about it. On the river, a barge full of scrap metal was pushed slowly upstream by a tug, the water foaming white across its blunt prow. Parker said, 'When does this boat get here?'

5

Claire said, 'What are you going to do?'

'Find out some things,' Parker told her. 'Talk to some people who might maybe like to come along. Take my time. It's at least three weeks before the boat opens for business.'

'There's something you don't like about it,' Claire said.

Parker got to his feet and started to pace. They were on the screened porch on the lake side of the house, the chitter of a light spring rain filling the silences around their words. The lake surface was pebbled, with little

21

irruptions where the breeze gusted. Usually the lake was quiet, glassy, reflecting the sky; now it was more like the river he'd been looking at yesterday.

'I don't like boats,' he said, pacing, looking out at the lake. 'To begin with. I don't like anything where there's one entrance, one exit. I don't like a cell. A boat on the water is a cell, you can't just get up and go away.'

'But the money,' she said.

'Cash.' He nodded. 'Cash is the hardest to find and the easiest to deal with. Anything else, you have to sell it, it's two transactions, not one. So the idea of the cash is good. But it's still cash on a boat. And besides that, there's Cathman.'

'What about him?'

'What does he want? Why is he doing this? There's something off-key there.'

'Male menopause.'

Parker did his barking laugh. 'He isn't chasing a fifteen-year-old girl,' he said, 'he's chasing a boat full of money. And he wants ten per cent. Ten per cent.'

'It's a finder's fee. *You'll* be doing all the work.'

'Why isn't he greedier? Why doesn't he want more? Why isn't he afraid we'll stiff him? Why does he have to tell me his thoughts about politics and gambling?'

'He's new to this,' she suggested. 'He's nervous, so he keeps talking.'

'Well, that's another thing that's wrong. He says he's got a perfect rep, nobody would think twice he could be linked up to something like this. So why is he? Why is he taking thirty years of straight narrow and tossing it in the wastebasket for ten per cent of something that might not happen? If he never thought this way, before, how can he think this way now? What's different in him?'

'Maybe he lied to you,' she said. 'Maybe he's not as clean as he says.'

'Then the cops will be on him the day after we pull the job, and what he has on me is a name and a phone number.' He stopped his pacing to look around the porch, and then at Claire. 'You want to move from here?'

'I like this house.'

He paced again, looking at nothing. 'I was thinking, when I was there, yesterday. There was an access road there, went down to the water, right next to the station, with a ramp at the bottom where you could launch a boat. I was thinking, there's nobody around, nobody even looking at the river, it's too early in the season. This guy knows two things about me, I could launch him right now, and come home, and forget it. All done.'

She winced a little at the idea, but said, 'Why didn't you?'

'Because he makes no sense,' he told her. He paced the porch as though he were in the cell he'd said he didn't like. 'I want to figure

23

him out. I want to know what's behind him, what he's doing, I want to know who he is, what he is, why he moves the way he does. Then I'll decide what to do about him.' He stopped in front of her, frowning down at her, thinking. 'You want to help?'

She blinked, and looked tense. 'You know,' she said, 'I don't like . . . there's things I don't like.'

'Nothing with trouble,' he promised. 'I've got the guy's calling card. You just spend some time in the library, spend some time on the phone. He'll have a paper trail. Get me a biography.'

'I could do that,' she agreed. 'And what will you be doing?'

'I'll go talk to a few guys,' Parker said.

6

'Edward Lynch,' Parker said, and extended a credit card with that name on it.

'Yes, sir, Mr Lynch,' the desk clerk said. She had a neat egg-shaped head with straight brown hair down both sides of it, like curtains at a window, and nothing much in the window. 'Pleasant trip?'

'Yes,' he said, and turned away from her canned chatter to look at the big echoing interior of the Brown Palace, Denver's finest, built around a great square atrium and furnished to let you know that you were in the western United States but that good taste prevailed. On the upper floors, all the rooms were on the far side of the halls, with a low wall on this side, overlooking the lobby. Here and there in the big space, groups of people sat in the low armchairs and sofas, leaning toward one another to talk things over, their words disappearing in the air. But a shotgun mike in any of the upper halls could pick up every conversation in the room.

'Here you are, Mr Lynch.'

Parker signed the credit card slip and took the plastic key. 'I think I have messages.'

She turned, as neatly articulated as a Barbie, and said, 'Yes, here we are. Two messages.' She slid the envelopes across the desk toward him. 'Will you want assistance with your luggage?'

'No, I'm okay.'

His luggage was one small brown canvas bag; he'd be here only one night. Picking the bag up, stuffing the message envelopes into his jacket pocket, he crossed to the elevators, not bothering to look out over the groups in the lobby. Mike and Dan wouldn't be there, they'd be waiting for his call, in their rooms.

You don't meet where you're going to pull the job, nowhere near it. And you don't meet anywhere that you've got a base or a drop or a contact or a home. Three days ago, just

25

after his conversation with Claire, Parker had started making phone calls, and when he made contact with the two guys he wanted he did a minimum of small talk and then said the same thing both times: 'I ran into Edward Lynch the other day. Remember him?' Both guys said yeah, they remembered Edward Lynch, what's he doing these days? 'Salesman, travels around the country. Said he was going to Denver, meet Bill Brown there on Thursday, then on and on, travel every which way. I'd hate that life.' Both guys agreed that Edward Lynch sure had it tough these days, and they did a little more nonsense talk, and hung up, and now it was Thursday and Parker was here as Edward Lynch, and he had the two messages in his pocket.

The room was a room, with a view of Denver, a city that's flat and broad. From a high floor like this, it looks tan, unmoving, a desert where people once used to live.

After Parker threw cold water on his face and unpacked his bag, he spread the two messages on the table beside the phone. Both gave him numbers here in the hotel. One was from Jack Strongarm and the other from Chuck Michaels. Jack Strongarm would be Dan Wycza, a big burly guy who was known to work as a professional wrestler when times were tough; the Strongarm moniker was what he used in the ring. Chuck Michaels would be Mike Carlow, a driver who was also a race-driver on the professional circuit; a madman on the track, but otherwise solid and reliable and sure.

Parker had no idea yet if this boat thing could be made to work, but if there was anything in it he'd need good pros to help put it together. He'd worked with both Wycza and Carlow more than once, and the best thing was, the last two times out with each of them everybody'd made a profit. So Wycza and Carlow would have good memories of Parker and reason to want to work with him again.

He called both message numbers, and both were answered by wary voices. 'Is this four twenty-nine?' he asked each time, since his room was 924, and both said no. He apologized twice, hung up, carried the bucket away to get ice, and when he was headed back he saw Mike Carlow coming the other way. A narrow rawboned guy in his forties, Carlow was a little shorter than medium height; good for fitting into those race cars. He had the leathery face and pale eyes of a man who spends a lot of time outdoors. His nose was long and narrow, lips thin, Adam's apple prominent. He got to 924 before Parker, and when Parker arrived he nodded and said, 'Hello, Parker. A long time since Tyler.' That was the last place they'd worked together. They'd all done well in Tyler, better than twenty-five thousand dollars a man. The memory gleamed in Carlow's pale eyes.

27

Parker unlocked them into the room. 'There's a bottle there, and the glasses, and here's ice.'

Looking at the glasses, Carlow said, 'Three of us.'

'Dan Wycza.'

'For the heavy lifting. Good.' Wycza had also been along in Tyler.

Carlow put an ice cube in a glass and poured enough bourbon to float it, then looked over at Parker, held up the bottle, and said, 'You?'

'The same,' Parker said, and someone knocked with a double rap. 'Make it two,' he said, and crossed to open the door.

Dan Wycza was a huge bald man with a handsome, playful face and heavy shoulders that he automatically shifted to an angle when he walked through doorways. He looked out at the world with amused mistrust, as though everybody he saw was an opponent in the wrestling ring who maybe couldn't be counted on to stick to the script. There was a rumor he was dead for a while, but then he'd popped up again. He was also known to be a health nut, which wouldn't keep him from accepting a glass of bourbon. He came in now, squared his shoulders, nodded a hello to Parker and said, 'Mike. Long time.'

'Tyler,' Carlow said, and brought Parker and Wycza their drinks.

'I spent that money,' Wycza said. Before

28

drinking, he looked at Parker: 'We gonna get some more?'

'Maybe. Sit down, let me describe it.'

There were two chairs in the room. Parker sat on the windowsill and said, 'It's cash. It's all in one place for several hours. I've got an inside man to give me the details. But there are maybe problems.'

Carlow said, 'Is the inside man one of the problems?'

'Don't know yet. Don't have him figured out. My woman's checking into him, his background, see what his story is.'

Wycza said, 'What does he say his story is?'

'Retired from state government, New York. Consultant to governments. Gave me his card.'

Wycza smiled in disbelief. 'He has a card?'

'He's legit, his whole life long. Got a reputation you could hang your overcoat on.'

Carlow said, 'So why's he giving you this score?'

'That's the question. But if it turns out he's all right, there's still problems, and the first one is, it's a boat.'

Carlow said, 'On the ocean?' The question he meant was: What do you want with a driver?

'On a river,' Parker told him. 'A gambling casino boat, a trial period, no gambling on credit, all cash, they take the cash off every six hours.'

'Not easy to leave a boat,' Wycza suggested,

29

'if all at once you want to.'

'That's part of the problem.'

Carlow said, 'How much cash?'

'The boat isn't running yet,' Parker said. 'So nobody knows what the take is. But a Friday night, five hours between ten P.M. and three A.M., it should be enough. I don't think the money's the problem, I think the boat's the problem.'

Wycza said, 'The boat isn't on that river now?'

'It's heading there. It used to be in Biloxi.'

Wycza grinned and said, 'The *Spirit of Biloxi*?'

'It's going to be the *Spirit of the Hudson* now. You know the boat?'

'You're giving me a chance to get my money back,' Wycza said. 'But, you know, they do heavy security on that boat. I did an automatic case when I was aboard, decided not to try it. They got rent-a-cops in brown everywhere you look. Cash goes straight down through a slot into some safe room down below. When you cash in your chips, they got a vacuum tube with little metal-like rockets in it, to send up just your money.'

Parker said, 'How about security when you're getting aboard?'

'Airport,' Wycza told him. 'You go through a metal detector. No X-ray, but they eyeball bags.'

'So no way to bring weapons aboard,'

30

Carlow said. 'Unless . . .' He looked at Wycza. 'Could you bring your own boat alongside?'

'Not without being seen. The dining rooms and other stuff is along the outside of the boat, gambling rooms inside. No windows when you gamble, windows all over the place when you eat a meal or have a drink or just sit around.'

'So that's the second problem,' Parker said. 'Guns. And the third problem is, getting the stuff off the boat.'

'And us,' Wycza said.

'That's the fourth problem,' Parker said.

Carlow said, 'The money's easy. Throw it overboard, in plastic. You got a boat trailing. That's me. I do boats as good as I do cars.'

Doubtful, Wycza said, 'They light up that boat pretty good.'

'A distraction at the front end,' Parker suggested. 'Maybe a fire. Nobody likes fire on a boat.'

Wycza said, '*I* don't like fire on a boat. And I also don't jump in a river in the dark and wait for Mike to come by and pick me up. Nothing against you, Mike.'

'I don't want people,' Carlow told him. 'Not with a boat. Plastic packages I can hook aboard and take off the other way.'

'We don't have this money yet,' Parker reminded him. 'To get it, we need a way to get guns aboard. We need a way to get into the room where they keep the money.'

Wycza said, 'This source of yours. Can he

give us blueprints?'

'When I told him I'd think about it,' Parker said, 'he gave me a whole package of stuff. Blueprints, schedules, staffing, I got it all.'

Carlow said, 'What does it say about guards? I'm wondering, are *we* guards, is that how we get the guns on board?'

'You mean, hijack some guards,' Wycza said, 'take their place. That's possible, it's been done sometimes.'

'I don't think so,' Parker said. 'You've got two security teams. Those rent-a-cops you saw when you were on the boat, they're hired by the private company owns the boat. They're regulars, they know each other. Down in the money room, the guards and the money counters are hired by the state government; they're a different bunch entirely. The way it's gonna work, a state bus picks them up, on a regular route, takes them to the boat all in a bunch, takes them home again the same way. They bring food from home, they don't get food on the boat. They're locked in at the start of their tour, unlocked again at the end when the money on their shift comes off the boat, surrounded by the money room crew plus armored car company guards.'

Carlow said, 'Maybe it isn't a boat job, maybe its an armored car job.'

'My inside man can only help me with the boat,' Parker said. 'In Albany, that's where the money comes off, it's like a three-block run from the dock to the bank, all city streets, heavily guarded.'

'Forget I said anything,' Carlow said. 'Anybody else want another?'

They did. Carlow distributed more ice and more bourbon, sat back down and said, 'We can't do a switch with the guards, the outer guards, the rent-a-cops. It wouldn't help us. Anyway, the big thing is, how do we get into the money room.'

'Parker's fire,' Wycza said. 'Set the fucking boat on fire, they'll open that door in a hurry.'

'I don't want to be on a burning boat,' Parker said. 'That wasn't the idea, about the fire, I just meant something small, to keep everybody looking forward when we do something at the back.'

'Three questions we got,' Carlow said. 'How do we get on, with the guns? How do we get into the money room? How do we get off again?'

Wycza said, 'Who can carry a gun on to the boat? Legit, I mean. The guards. Anybody else?'

'A cop,' Parker said. 'An off-duty cop, he could be carrying, they'd probably leave him alone.'

'Maybe,' Wycza said. 'Or maybe they'd be very polite, thank you, sir, if you don't mind, sir, we'll just check this weapon for you until you leave the boat, sir. They're not gonna let people carry guns unless there's a reason.'

'Bodyguards,' Carlow suggested, and turned to Wycza to say, 'Does this boat have entertainment? Shows? Would celebrities come aboard?'

'They got shows,' Wycza said, 'but not what you'd call headliners. Not people you been reading about in the *National Enquirer.*'

'Bodyguards,' Parker said. 'There might be something there. Wait, let me think.' He turned his head to look out the window at tan Denver.

Wycza said to Carlow, 'You been racin' much?'

'I totaled a Lotus at a track in Tennessee,' Carlow told him. 'Broke my goddam leg again, too. I need a stake to build a new car.'

'I gotta quit wrestlin' for a while,' Wycza said. 'I get tired of bein' beat up by blonds. In capes, a lot of them.'

Parker turned back. 'Either of you know a guy named Lou Sternberg?'

Wycza frowned, then shook his head. Carlow said, 'Maybe. One of us?'

'Yes.'

'Lives some funny place.'

'London.'

'That's it.'

Wycza said, 'An Englishman?'

Parker told him, 'American, but he lives over there. Only he never works there, he always comes to the States when he needs a bankroll.'

'He was on a bank thing I drove,' Carlow said. 'In Iowa. Jeez, seven, eight years ago. I came in late, the guy they had first got grabbed on a parole violation, so I didn't get to know the rest of the string very much. Just the guy, Mackey, that brought me in.'

'Ed Mackey,' Wycza said. 'Him we all know. Him and Brenda.'

Carlow said to Parker, 'What about Sternberg?'

'Remember what he looks like? How he talks?'

'Sure. Heavyset, sour most of the time, talks like a professor.'

'Can you see him,' Parker said, 'as a state legislator? One of the anti-gambling crowd, coming for an inspection.'

Wycza laughed. 'And we're his fucking bodyguards!' he said.

Carlow said, 'An assemblyman, with bodyguards? Are you sure?'

'He's had death threats,' Wycza explained. 'Cause he's such an uncompromising guy. So he's got us to guard him.'

'Armed to the teeth,' Parker said.

7

'Hello?'

'I'm looking for Lou Sternberg.'

'Oh, I'm sorry, he's gone out, May I tell him who rang?'

'Ed Lynch.'

'Does he know the subject, Mr Lynch?'

'Not yet, not until I tell him.'

'Does he know *you*, Mr Lynch?'

'We were in the art business together one time. Buying and selling art.'

'Oh, I believe he's mentioned that. It wasn't a very profitable business, was it, Mr Lynch?'

'No profit at all.'

'And are you still in the art business, Mr Lynch?'

'No, I gave that up.'

'Probably just as well. What business are you in now, Mr Lynch?'

'Politics . . . Hello?'

'You surprise me, Mr Lynch.'

'Things change.'

'So I see. May I ask— Forgive me, but I know Mr Sternberg will ask *me*, so I should know the answers.'

'That's okay. I thought he might like to run for state assemblyman.'

'Mr Sternberg?'

'Yes.'

'But— Mr Sternberg lives in London.'

'That's where I'm calling him.'

'Wouldn't he have to be resident in the United States?'

'For a little while.'

'Oh, I see. This wouldn't be a full term, then. Completing someone else's term, something like that.'

'Something like that. My friends and me, we think Mr Sternberg has the right look, he could inspire confidence in people.'

'Probably so. Well, I have no idea if Mr Sternberg would be interested. May I have him ring you when he gets in?'

'When would that be?'

'I expect him, oh, in ten minutes.'

'I'm calling from the States.'

'Yes, I assumed that.'

'The number here's two oh one five five five nine nine one three.'

'And is that a business or residence?'

'It's a gas station.'

'Ah. Petrol, we call it here. If Mr Sternberg is interested, he'll ring you within fifteen minutes. If he doesn't ring back by then, you'll know he isn't interested'

'We say "call back" here.'

'Yes, I know. Goodbye, Mr Lynch.'

*   *   *

Parker sat in the car next to the phone booth

and watched the customers pump their own gas, then pay the clerk in the bulletproof glass booth. Nine minutes later, the phone rang.

8

Claire made meals for herself when Parker was away, but when he was at home they always ate out. 'You wouldn't want what I eat when I'm here by myself,' she told him once. 'No man would think it was dinner.' So they'd drive somewhere and eat.

Tonight's place was competent and efficient and, like a lot of country restaurants, too brightly lit. Claire waited until the waitress had brought their main courses, and then she talked about Cathman: 'He's a bureaucrat. He's exactly what he says he is.'

'Then he doesn't make any sense,' Parker said, and carved at his steak.

Claire took a small notebook from her bag and opened it on the table beside her plate. 'He's sixty-three,' she said. 'He has an engineering degree from Syracuse University, and his entire adult life he's worked for state government in New York. He was in some sort of statistical section for years, and then he moved on to fiscal planning. Two years ago, he retired, though he didn't have to. I think what it is, he disagreed with state policy.'

'About what?'

'Gambling.'

Parker nodded. 'That's where it is,' he said. 'Whatever's thrown him out of whack, the gambling thing is where it is.'

'You mean that would make him change his spots.'

'Change the whole coat.'

Claire sipped at her wine, and said, 'Maybe he needs money after all. A mid-level civil servant, retired early, maybe it's rougher than he thought it would be.'

'What about this consultant business?'

Claire shook her head. She sliced duck breast, thinking about it, then said, 'I don't think it's doing all that well. Mostly I think because he's advising state governments against gambling and they're all in favor of it.'

'He told me about that,' Parker agreed. 'The pols see it as painless taxes.'

'People don't want you to consult with them,' Claire said, 'if you're only going to advise them not to do what they've already decided they're going to do. So what jobs he gets, mostly, have to do with fund allocation for mass transit and highways and airports. Here and there, he gets a job doing research for anti-gambling groups in state legislatures, but not that much.'

The music in here was noodling jazz piano, low enough to talk over but loud enough for privacy. Still, when the waitress spent time

39

clearing the main course dishes from the next table, Parker merely ate his steak and drank some of his wine. When she left, he said, 'But he isn't in it for the money, I don't think. The thing with me, I mean.'

Claire nodded, watching him.

Parker thought back to his dealings with Cathman. 'It doesn't *feel* like it,' he said, 'as though money's the point. That's part of what's wrong with him. If it isn't money he wants, what *does* he want?'

'You could still walk away,' she said.

'I might. Bad parts to it. Still, it's cash, that means something.'

'The boat isn't even here yet,' she pointed out. 'You still have plenty of time to be sure about him, learn more about him.'

'You do that,' Parker told her. 'His home life now. Wife, girlfriend, children, whatever he's got. People bend each other; is anybody bending Cathman?'

'You want me to do that?'

'Yes.'

Claire nodded. 'All right,' she said, and ate a bit, and then said, 'What will you be doing?'

'The river,' Parker said.

9

It was called the Lido, but it shouldn't have been. It was an old bar, a gray wood cube cut deep into the ground floor of a narrow nineteenth-century brick house, and at two on a sunny afternoon in April it was dark and dry, smelling of old whiskey and dead wood. The shirtsleeved bald bartender was tall and fat, looking like a retired cop who'd gone to seed the day his papers had come through. At the bar, muttering together about sports and politics—other people's victories and defeats—were nine or ten shabbily dressed guys who were older than their teeth.

Not looking at any of them, Parker went to the corner of the long bar nearest the door, sat on the stool there, and when the barman plodded down to him like the old bull he was, he ordered beer. The muttering farther along the bar faltered for a minute, while they all tried to work out what this new person meant, but Parker did nothing of interest, so they went back to their conversations.

Parker paid for his beer, drank it, and left, and outside the sunlight seemed a hundred per cent brighter. Squinting, he walked down the half block to the Subaru he was still driving —no reason not to, and he'd dump it after the job, if the job happened—and leaned against its trunk in the sunlight.

He was in Hudson today, a town along the river of the same name, another twenty miles north and upstream from Rhinecliff, where he'd met Cathman at the railroad station. The town stretched up a long gradual slope from the river, with long parallel streets lined like stripes up the hill. At the bottom was a slum where there used to be a port, back in the nineteenth century, when the whalers came this far up the Hudson with their catch to the plants beside the river where the whale oil and blubber and other sellable materials were carved and boiled and beaten out of the cadavers, to be shipped to the rest of America along the Erie Canal and the Great Lakes and the midwest rivers.

The whalers and the whale industry and the commercial uses of the waterways were long gone, but the town was still here. It had become poor, and still was. At one point, early in the twentieth century, it was for a while the whorehouse capital of the northeast, and less poor, until a killjoy state government stepped in to make it virtuous and poor again. Now it was a drug distribution hub, out of New York City via road or railroad, and for the legitimate world it was an antiques center.

The Lido was just about as far from the water as it could get and still be on one of the streets that came up from the river. Where Parker waited in the sunlight he couldn't see the river at all, just the old low buildings in two rows stretched away along the upper flat and then downslope. Being poor for so long, Hudson hadn't seen much modernization, and so, without trying, had become quaint.

About two minutes later, one of the shabby guys came out of the Lido, looked around, saw Parker, and walked toward him. He looked to be about fifty, but grizzled and gray beyond his years, as though at one time he'd gone through that whale factory and all the meat and juice had been pressed out of him. His thin hair was brown and dry, his squinting eyes a pale blue, his cheeks stubble-grown. He was in nondescript gray-and-black workclothes, and walked with the economical shuffle Parker recognized; this fellow, probably more than once in his life, had been on the yard.

Which made sense. To find this guy, Parker had made more phone calls, saying he wanted somebody who knew the river and could keep his mouth shut. Most of the people he'd called were ex-cons, and most of the people they knew were ex-cons, so why wouldn't this guy be?

He stopped in front of Parker, reserved, watchful, waiting it out. He said, 'Lynch?'

'Hanzen?'

'That's me,' Hanzen agreed. 'I take it you know a friend of mine.'

'Pete Rudd.'

'Pete it is,' Hanzen said. 'What do you hear

43

from Pete?'

'He's out.'

Hanzen grinned, showing very white teeth. 'We're all out,' he said. 'This your car?'

'Come on along.'

They got into the Subaru, Parker pulled away from the curb, and Hanzen said, 'Take the right.'

'We're not going to the river?'

'Not in town, there's nothing down there but jigs. Little ways north.'

They drove for twenty minutes, Hanzen giving the route, getting them out of town on to a main road north, then left on to a county road. Other than Hanzen's brief directions, there was silence in the car. They didn't know one another and, in any case, neither of them was much for small talk.

From the county road, Hanzen told Parker to take the left on to a dirt road between a crumbled barn and a recently plowed field with some green bits coming up. 'Corn later,' he said, nodding at the field; his only bit of tour guiding.

This dirt road twisted downward around the end of the cornfield and through scrubby trees and undergrowth where the land was too steep for ready plowing. Then it leveled, and they bumped across railroad tracks, and Parker said, 'Amtrak?'

'They always yell when they're comin,' Hanzen said.

44

Just beyond the tracks, the road widened into an oval dirt area where a lot of cars had parked at one time or another and a number of fires had been laid. Low ailanthus and tall maples crowded in on the sides, and the river was right there, at the far end of the dirt oval. Its bottom was mud and stone, quickly dropping off. To the left, downstream, three decayed and destroyed small boats lay half in and half out of the water. One of them was partly burned. About ten feet from the bank a gray outboard motorboat pulled at its mooring in the downriver current. A roughmade low windowless cabin painted dark blue covered the front half of the boat.

Parker and Hanzen got out of the car. Hanzen took off his shoes, socks and pants, rolled them in a bundle and put them on the ground. He wore white jockey shorts that bagged on him, as though they'd been washed too many times. He waded out into the water, grabbed the anchor line, and pulled the boat close, then untied the line from the float and used the line to tow the boat to shore, saying as he came in, 'I got to keep it out there or the kids come and shoot up in it.' Pointing, 'Set it on fire, like that one.'

'Nothing's easy,' Parker said.

'Amen,' Hanzen said. He waded out of the water, pulling the boat after him until the prow scraped on dry land, then pulled on the side of the boat until it came around far enough that the deck behind the cabin was reachable from the bank. 'Climb aboard,' he said.

Parker stepped over the gunwale. The interior was recently painted, gray, and very neat. Two solid wood doors were closed over the cabin, with a padlock.

'Take this stuff, will you?' Hanzen said, holding out the roll of his clothes, and Parker took them and put them on the deck next to the cabin door, while Hanzen pushed the boat off again from shore until it floated, then climbed over the side. 'Give me a minute,' he said.

'Go ahead.'

Hanzen unrolled his pants, found a ring of keys, and unlocked the padlock on the cabin. He pulled the doors open, and Parker got a look at a narrow lumpy bunk under a dark brown blanket, some wooden boxes and cardboard cartons used as shelves and storage, and Playboy bunnies on the inside of the cabin doors. Then Hanzen stooped inside, found a towel, dried his legs, tossed the towel in on the bunk, shut but didn't lock the doors, and dressed himself. Only then did he go to the wheel beside the cabin doors, put the key in the ignition, and start the motor.

By then they'd drifted a ways south and out into the stream. There was no place to sit, so Parker stood on the other side of the cabin doors from Hanzen and the wheel, put one forearm on the cabin top, and looked at the bank. As they floated farther from shore, he could see other landings north and south, a few old structures, some small boats at anchorage. There was no apparent commerce, and he didn't see anything that looked like vacation settlements or estates.

Hanzen said, 'It's north you care about, right?'

'Yes.'

Hanzen turned the wheel, and goosed the motor, and their slow drift backward became a steadily increasing push forward. Wake hissed along the sides. 'We'll go up this bank, down the other,' Hanzen said. He had to speak a little louder now.

They rode in silence for about five minutes. There were no boats around at all, though Parker knew there was still some barge traffic sometimes along here, and in summer there would be the pleasure boaters, both sail and motor. But off-season the river wasn't used much.

They were keeping close to the east bank, and it stayed pretty much the same until they passed another river town, smaller than Hudson, and looking poorer, its clapboard houses climbing above one another back up the hill from the water. Hanzen steered farther away from shore at that point, out closer to the middle of the river, which was very wide here, the other bank visible but not clear, just a blur of green and the colors of structures.

North of that town, Hanzen steered closer to the bank again and said, 'You don't mind, I got some stuff of my own to look at along here.'

'Go ahead.'

'First we see if my alarm's okay,' Hanzen said, and steered abruptly leftward, toward the middle of the river, so that Parker had to press his forearm down on the cabin top to keep his balance. Hanzen drove out a ways, then swung around in a wide half-circle, looking toward the shore, and smiled in satisfaction. 'There it is,' he said. 'You see the big branch bent down?'

Parker shook his head. 'Just so you do,' he said.

Hanzen grinned at him. 'That's right, I guess. We know what we have to know, and we see what we have to see.'

Parker said, 'What is this branch?'

'I've got some stuff in there,' Hanzen said. 'Nobody's gonna bother it except law. If the law finds it, they're gonna touch it, probably pull it outa there. The minute they do, the minute they touch it at all or come at it the wrong way, that big tree branch I got tied so it bends down, it'll release and go right back up. I come here, I don't see my branch bent down, I just drive on by. Happened to me once, three years ago. Not here, another place.'

What Hanzen was doing here, Parker knew, was showing his credentials, his qualifications,

48

should it be that Parker might have further use for him and want to know what sort of man he was. Because all they had between them so far was that Parker would give him three hundred dollars for a tour of the river north of Hudson up toward Albany, and more money if he was needed for anything else later. The subject of this trip was not for Hanzen to worry about, and the trip was not for him to talk about with anybody else. But of course he had to know something was being planned here, and wonder if maybe they could use a trustworthy river man later on.

Maybe. Time would tell.

As they neared shore, Hanzen slowed the boat to an easy glide, so the prow was no longer lifted and they left barely a ripple of wake. Ahead of them was a stretch of undeveloped bank, tangled with undergrowth. Large tree branches reached out over the water. It would be almost impossible to get to the bank anywhere along here, and probably just as tough to get to the water from the other side. Whatever Hanzen was hiding, he'd picked a good spot for it.

'There they are. My babies.' Hanzen grinned with fatherly pride. 'See?'

There were about a dozen of them, widely spaced along the shoreline, under the overhanging branches, and it took Parker a minute to figure out what they were. Fifty-pound sacks of peat moss. Facing upward, they

49

hung just barely above the water, suspended from strong-test fishing line fastened to all four corners of each bag and to strong free limbs above. In each bag, two long slits had been cut along the upper side, and marijuana planted in the peat moss through the slits. The young leaves were bright acrylic green, hardy and healthy. The bags and their crop received filtered sunlight through the trees, but would be invisible from just about anywhere, including low-flying aircraft. You'd have to steer in here from the river to see them, and even then you pretty well had to already know they existed or you probably wouldn't notice.

'We're a long way from the ocean,' Hanzen said, steering slowly along beside his babies, looking them over, 'but we still get the tidal effect. Twice a day, they get a good long drink of water.'

'Nice setup,' Parker agreed.

'My only problem is, if somebody steals a boat,' Hanzen said. 'Then you got deputies in their launch, poking in places like this, looking for the goddam boat, and finding all this. Happened once, could happen again. In the fall, maybe, a fisherman might anchor in here, do some fly-casting out into the current, but by then I'm harvested and out of here.'

'You got much of this?'

'Sixty bags, up and down the river. Little farther on, there's one more batch I want to check, that's all in this direction.' Hanzen smiled out at the empty river. 'You can really be alone out here, if you want,' he said. 'If you know what you're doing out here, the world's your oyster.'

'I suppose so.'

Hanzen studied Parker. 'You don't like rivers,' he decided. 'Water, whatever. But you're doing something, and right now you need the river, so I guess what you're looking for's a place to go out from the bank, or come ashore, or both. I'd be happier if you didn't use my place down there.'

'I need to be farther north,' Parker told him.

'Closer to Albany,' Hanzen suggested, 'but not all the way to Albany.'

'Right.'

'And you'd like to mark it, and not tell me which spot you picked.' Hanzen grinned. 'That's okay, I understand. Only it won't work.'

'No?'

'Things look different from the land,' Hanzen explained. 'From out here, you could pick the spot you want, but when you get on shore you'll never find it.'

'Not without you, you mean,' Parker said.

'Not without somebody knows the river,' Hanzen said.

'Somebody I trust,' Parker said.

Hanzen grimaced again; things didn't bother him much. 'You're already trusting me,' he said, 'out here on my boat, even though that's a little .22 under your shirt. Come on,

51

let's head upriver, and you sing out when you
see something you like.'

10

They spent three hours on the river, and there
were four spots along the way that Parker
thought he might be interested in, three on the
east shore and one on the west. Hanzen had
road maps in his cabin that showed this part of
the river, and he pointed out to Parker where
each potential spot was, so he could see what
road access he'd have, and what towns were
nearby.

From time to time, as they moved, long low
barges went slowly past, upriver or down, piled
with boxed cargo or with trash. The crews
waved, and Hanzen waved back, and each time
their smaller boat rocked from side to side in
the long slow undulations of the barge's wake,
no matter how far off to the side they were.

They also saw, at one point on the way
back, as they hugged the more thickly settled
western shore, a fast speedboat, white with
blue trim, heading downriver across the way,
close to the opposite bank. A police launch.
'Stay away from my babies, now,' Hanzen told
it.

Parker said, 'They patrol much?'

'Not at all,' Hanzen said. 'Not enough

activity on the river to keep them out here regular. They'll come out for the fun of it, sometimes, in the daylight, but at night they only come out if there's a problem.' Nodding at Parker, he said, 'You can count on it, though, if there's a problem, they will come out.'

'All right,' Parker said.

A while later, Hanzen said, 'Seen enough?'

Parker looked around. 'We're back?'

'That's my mooring,' Hanzen said, pointing across the river, where nothing specific could be seen. 'I don't think you care about anything south of this.'

'No, you're right.'

'You might as well pay me now.'

Parker took the envelope out of his hip pocket and handed it over. Hanzen squeezed it enough so the slit opened and he could see the edges of the twenties. Satisfied, he pulled open one cabin door long enough to toss the envelope on to the bunk. 'Nice doing business with you, Mr Lynch,' he said. 'Maybe we'll do it again sometime.'

'Maybe,' Parker agreed.

As Hanzen steered them across the wide river, Parker held the map down on the cabin top and studied the possibilities. If it seemed like the job would work out, Mike Carlow would come here and look over the routes, see which one he liked best, which one fitted in with whatever way they decided to work it.

When they were more than halfway across, with the current slapping hard at the left side of the boat, Parker could begin to see the dark red color of the Subaru straight ahead, parked just up from the water. He could see people, too, three of them, in dark clothing. And two or three motorcycles. 'You've got visitors,' he said.

Hanzen nodded. 'Friends of mine. And you're just Mr Lynch, a man looking for a place to put a restaurant with a river view.'

'Here's your map,' Parker said.

'Put it in the cabin,' Hanzen told him, so Parker opened a cabin door and dropped the map in on to the bunk next to the envelope of twenties, then shut the door again.

Hanzen slowed as they neared the shore, and Parker looked over at the three of them waiting there. Bikers. Two were heavyset middle-aged men with heavy beards and mean eyes and round beerguts; the third was younger, thinner, clean-shaven. All were in leather jackets and jeans. The two older ones sat on the ground, backs against their motorcycles, while the third, jittery, hopped-up, kept walking this way and that in the little clearing, watching the approaching boat, talking to the other two, looking back up the road they'd all come down. Finally, one of the older men spoke to the young one, who agreed and came down to the water's edge to wait for the boat.

54

Hanzen steered carefully forward, and the young biker leaned way out over the water to grab the prow. As he pulled the boat partway up on to the bank, Hanzen again stripped out of shoes and socks and pants, and rolled them in a ball. 'Ernie!' he called, and the young biker, who had a face like a white crow, with smallpox, looked alert. 'Catch!'

Hanzen tossed his bundle of clothes, and Ernie caught it like a football, with both forearms and belly. The other two bikers laughed, and Ernie turned around, jumpy, with a twitchy grin, to pretend to throw a forward pass. One shoe fell out of the bundle on to the ground, near the water.

Hanzen, sounding more bored than irritated, called, 'Don't fuck around, Ernie, you don't want to get my shoe wet. Pull the boat round sideways so Mr Lynch can get off.'

Ernie hustled to pick up the shoe, carry it and the bundle farther from the water, put them down, and hurry back to pull the boat around at an angle to the bank.

Parker said, 'See you around.'

'Anytime,' Hanzen said. 'You know where I am.' He stuck out his hand and Parker shook it, then climbed over the side on to the bank.

The older bikers watched with slow interest as Parker walked toward the Subaru. Behind him, at Hanzen's continuing orders, Ernie pushed the boat free of the shore, apparently getting his own feet wet in the process, and that was good for a general laugh.

Parker got into the Subaru. Offshore, Hanzen was tying the anchor line to the float. Parker started the Subaru, backed in a half-circle, shifted into drive, and saw that one of the bikes, with its owner seated leaning against it, was in his way. He drove forward and put his foot on the brake, and the biker pretended not to see him, to be interested in watching Hanzen wade ashore.

Parker leaned his head out the Subaru window: 'You care about that bike?'

The biker turned his head. He contemplated Parker for a long minute, unmoving, and just as Parker took his foot off the brake he grunted and struggled to his feet and wheeled the bike out of the way.

Hanzen was on shore now, drying his legs with a towel Ernie had brought him from his own bike's saddlebag. Parker completed his turn to the dirt road and jounced over the railroad track.

They all watched him go.

11

Claire had her own car, a gray Lexus, legitimately registered in her name at the Colliver Pond address. She'd driven off in it three days ago, to look into Hilliard Cathman's private life, so when Parker heard the garage door opener switch on at three that afternoon it was probably Claire coming back. But it didn't have to be Claire coming back.

Parker had been seated in the living room, looking at maps of New York State, and now he reached under the sofa to close his hand on the S&W .32 revolver stored there. He tugged, and the clip holding the revolver gave a small metallic click, and the .32 nestled into his hand.

He rose, crossed the living room and hall and the kitchen, looked through the hole he'd drilled a long time ago at eye level in the door between kitchen and garage, and saw the Lexus drive in, this side of the Subaru already parked in there. Claire was alone in the car, and didn't seem troubled by anything. He watched her reach up to the visor to lower the garage door behind her.

When Claire walked into the living room, Parker was again studying the maps. The revolver wasn't in sight. He looked up and said, 'Welcome back.'

She nodded at the maps. 'Planning a trip?'

'You tell me.'

'Ah.' She smiled and nodded. 'You can keep them open, I guess. After I shower and you bring me a drink, I'll tell you all about it.

*   *   *

It was nearly six when they got around to talking, the long spring twilight just starting to stretch its fingers outside the house. Claire sat up in bed, back against the headboard, a sheet partly over her. Her drink, the ice cubes long gone, she held on her upbent knee, the tan skin looking browner against the clear glass. Parker, in black trousers, paced as he listened.

She said, 'Cathman's a widower, his wife died of cancer seven years ago. No girlfriends. Three grown daughters, all married, living in different parts of the northeast. Everybody gets along all right, but they're not a close-type family. At Christmas he'll go to a daughter's house, that's about it.'

'He's alone?'

'He lives alone. In the two-room office he's got for his consulting business, he has a secretary, an older woman named Rosemary Shields. She worked with him for years when he was with state government, she retired when he did, kept working for him. She's one of those devoted secretaries where there's never been sex but she'd kill for him and he wouldn't know how to live without her.'

'He has to know other people,' Parker said. He frowned out the window at the lake, where it now reflected the start of sunset, as though a lot of different pastel paints had been spilled on it. 'He isn't a loner,' he said.

'Not by choice,' Claire agreed. She sipped at her drink and said, 'He's always

58

been a bureaucrat, his friends have always been other bureaucrats. They all got older together, retired, died off, moved away. He's in correspondence with a couple of people in Florida, one in California. He still knows a few people around Albany, but doesn't hang out with them much. When he wants to see somebody in his office on business, the guy is usually in for him.'

Parker touched the window glass; it was cool. He said, 'Money?'

'His retirement. The consulting business brings in a little, not much. He's lived in the same house for thirty-four years, in a suburb called Delmar, paid off the mortgage a long time ago.'

'Protégés? Young bureaucrats coming up?'

'He's on the wrong side of the issue,' she said. 'Or he's got the wrong issues. And he was never important enough to cultivate. I think basically people are ready to forget him, except he's still around here and there. Comes to the testimonial dinners and the news conferences.'

'Brothers, sisters?'

'Two older brothers, both dead. Some cousins and nephews and nieces he never sees. He comes from two old New England families; his first name, Hilliard, was his mother's maiden name. Anglican ministers and college professors.'

Parker nodded, then turned to offer Claire his thin smile. 'That's why the anti-gambling.'

'His forebears would turn in their graves.'

'Armed robbery,' Parker said. 'They'd spin a little for that one, too, wouldn't they?'

'I'd think so,' Claire agreed.

Parker turned back to the window. The spilled paint on the lake was getting darker. He said, 'He'll think about those forebears, won't he? He'll want to make it right, not upset them a lot.'

Claire watched his profile and said nothing.

After a minute, Parker shook his head in irritation. 'I don't like wasted motion,' he said. 'But I just have the feeling, before this is over, I'm gonna have to put Cathman out of his misery.'

12

Rosemary Shields was as Claire had described her: a rotund older woman with iron-gray hair in an iron arrangement of tight coils close to her head. She escaped an air of the maternal by dressing in browns and blacks, and by maintaining a manner of cold clerical efficiency. When Parker entered her office through the frosted glass door that read:

1100
Hilliard Cathman Associates

in gold letters, she was briskly typing at her computer keyboard, making sounds like crickets in the walls. She stopped the crickets and looked up with some surprise; not many people came through that door. But Parker had dressed for the part, in dark suit and white shirt and low-key striped tie, so she wouldn't be alarmed.

'Yes?' she asked, unable to hide the surprise, and he knew she mostly expected to hear he'd come to the wrong office.

Parker shut the door. The hall had been empty, the names on the other frosted glass doors along here describing law firms, accountants, 'media specialists' and 'consultants.' Camp followers of state government. 'Cathman,' Parker said.

Surprise gave way to that natural efficiency: 'Yes, of course,' as she reached for the phone. 'Is Mr Cathman expecting you?'

Was Cathman expecting anybody? Parker went along with the fiction that business was being done here, saying, 'Tell him it's Mr Lynch. Tell him I'm with the Parkers.'

'Yes, sir,' she said, and tapped the intercom button on the phone.

While she murmured into the phone, not quite studying him out of the corners of her eyes as she spoke with Cathman, Parker looked around at the office. It was small and square and without windows, the walls lined with adjustable bookshelves full of law books

61

and technical journals. The one clear area of wall space, behind Rosemary Shields' desk, contained a pair of four-drawer filing cabinets and, above them, a large framed reproduction of Ben Shahn's Sacco and Vanzetti poster. So Cathman was not a man to give up a cause just because it was dead.

Rosemary Shields hung up: 'He'll be right out.'

'Thank you.'

And he was. Parker turned toward the inner door, and it opened. Cathman stuck his head out, like a mole out of his hole in the ground, not sure what he was going to see, and relief showed clearly on his face when he saw it was Parker out there. Fortunately, his Rosemary had gone back to her computer keyboard and didn't see her boss's face. Or was she in on it, along for Cathman's U-turn into crime? Parker doubted it, but there was no way to be sure.

'Oh, yes,' Cathman said. 'Mr Lynch, of course. Come in, please.'

Parker followed him into the inner office, and Cathman shut the door, his manner switching at once to a fussy indignation. 'Mr Parker,' he half-whispered, in a quick high-pitched stutter. 'You shouldn't come here like this. It's too dangerous.'

'Not for me,' Parker told him, and looked around at Cathman's lair. It was a larger office than the one outside, but not by much. One wall was mostly window, with a view out and down toward the huge dark stone pile of the statehouse, a turreted medieval castle, outsize and grim, built into the steep slope and now surrounded by the scuttle of modern life. From here, you saw the statehouse from an angle behind it and farther up the hill—and from the eleventh floor—and the steep city in a tumble of commercial and government buildings on down to the river.

Inside here, Cathman had made a nest for himself, with an imposing partner's desk-inset green felt top, a kneehole and drawers on both sides so the partners could sit facing one another—angled into a corner, where Cathman could look out the window and still face the door. There were more bookcases in here, but better ones, freestanding, with glass doors that closed down over each shelf. Framed diplomas and testimonials and photos were spaced around the walls. An L-shaped sofa in dark red and a dark wood coffee table filled the corner opposite the desk.

Cathman, calmed by Parker's indifference, but still feeling wronged, came forward, making impatient brushing gestures at the sofa. 'Yes, well, at least you used a different name,' he said. 'Sit down, sit down, as long as you're here. But I already told you, I repeatedly told you, I'll be happy to meet you anywhere, anywhere at all, answer any questions you have, just phone me and—'

63

'Sit down,' Parker said.

They were on opposite sides of the coffee table. Cathman blinked, looked at the sofa, looked at Parker, and said, 'My secretary—'

'Rosemary Shields.'

Cathman blinked again, then thought, and then nodded. 'Yes, you do your research. You probably know all there is to know about me by now.'

'Not all,' Parker said.

'Well, the point is,' Cathman said, 'Miss Shields will expect me to offer you a cold drink. We're not equipped to do coffee here, but we have a variety of soft drinks and seltzer and so on in the refrigerator under her desk. Business meetings begin with that, she'll expect it. What would you like? I can recommend the Saratoga water, it's a New York State mineral water, very good.'

The local politician to the end. Parker said, 'Sure, I'll try it.'

'*Please* sit down.'

Parker sat on the side of the sofa where the light from the window would be behind him. Easier then to see Cathman's face, harder for Cathman to see his. Meanwhile, Cathman went back to the door, opened it, murmured to Miss Shields, shut the door, and returned. 'She'll bring it, in just a moment.'

'So this is the time we talk about the weather, right?'

Cathman smiled, apparently surprising

64

himself when he did it. 'I doubt that,' he said, 'though it would be usual, yes. But we won't want to discuss— Ah, Miss Shields. Thank you.'

They waited and watched her in silence as she brought in a small silver tray, on which faintly jingled two bottles of mineral water and two glasses with ice cubes. She didn't speak, but continued her performance of being in a world where her efficiency mattered. She put the tray on the coffee table, nodded to Cathman, and left, closing the door firmly but quietly behind her.

Cathman actually wanted water; he poured himself some as he said, 'Is there really any reason for this urgency?'

'No urgency,' Parker told him. 'I wanted to talk to you, and I wanted to see your place.'

'And now you've seen it. Will you need to see it again?'

'I hope not.'

Cathman sipped his bubbly water, put the glass down, and gave Parker a curious look. 'That was some sort of threat, wasn't it? What you meant was, the only reason you'd come back here is if you intended to do me harm.'

Parker said, 'Why would I want to do you harm?'

'Only if I'd done you some.' Cathman smiled. 'And I'm not going to, so that's an end to that. Mr Parker, I do understand what sort of man you are, I really do. I knew what sort of

65

man our late friend Marshall Howell was. I am no threat to you, nor to anybody at all except the gambling interests in New York State.'

'That's nice,' Parker said.

'You wanted to—'

'Talk to you about those gambling interests,' Parker told him, 'and the people opposed to them. There's some state legislators against it, right?'

'In a minority, I'm afraid.'

'That's a list you'll have.'

Cathman was startled. 'You want a list of anti-gambling legislators? But, why would you want to— You don't mean to *approach* them.'

'Cathman,' Parker said, 'get the list.'

Cathman didn't know what to do. He needed reassurance, but if Parker were to consult with him once, give him explanations, then Cathman would want explanations and reassurances all the time. Stop it now, and it's dealt with.

When Cathman couldn't stand the silence any more, he put down his glass of New York State mineral water, with a *click* on the coffee table, louder than he'd intended, and said, 'I'll get—But— Of course, it can't leave— Well.'

Parker watched him. Finally Cathman got to his feet and hurried from the room.

There was a second door in here, narrower, in the other corner, farthest from the desk. A way out, or a bathroom? Parker rose and crossed over there, and it was a bathroom, small and efficient, with a shower. Towels were hung askew, the soap in the shower was a smallish stub, hotel shampoos were on the shelf in there; so it was used, from time to time.

As Parker headed back toward the sofa, Cathman returned, a thick manila folder in his hand. He saw Parker in motion, looked quickly at his desk, then realized Parker was coming from the other direction, and stopped worrying; about that, anyway.

When they were both seated, Cathman put the folder on his lap, rested a protective hand on it, and said, 'If you could tell me what you want . . .'

'An anti-gambling legislator. Not from this part of the state. Short and fat. Sour expression.'

Cathman looked alert, ready to be of help. 'Do you know his name?'

'You're going to tell me,' Parker said. 'He should be an obscure guy, somebody most people wouldn't know very much.'

'Oh, I see,' Cathman said, and shook his head. 'I'm sorry, I was confused, I thought you meant one specific person, but you want a *type*, someone to match a— Well, it would have to be an assemblyman, not a state senator, if you want someone obscure. There are many more assemblymen than senators.'

'How many assemblymen?'

'One hundred and fifty.'

'That's a good herd,' Parker said. 'Cut me out one. Short and fat. Sour expression. Most people don't know him, or wouldn't recognize him.'

'Let me see.' Cathman opened the folder, riffled through the sheets of paper in there, then found it was more comfortable to put the folder on the coffee table and bend over it. After a minute, he looked up and said, 'Would New York City be all right?'

'Wouldn't they be well known?'

'Not at all. There are sixty assemblymen from New York City alone. And assemblywomen, of course.' Cathman shrugged. 'And to tell the truth,' he said, 'the rural people and the people in towns are likelier to know their assemblyman than the people down in the city.'

'What have you got?'

'His name is Morton Kotkind, from Brooklyn. His district has hospitals and colleges, a lot of transients. It always has among the lowest percentage of eligible voters who actually cast the ballot. Nobody actually *likes* Kotkind, he's just a good obedient party man who does the job, and it's a safe seat there, where nobody will ever notice him.'

'Sounds good.'

'He's a lawyer, of course, they're all lawyers. He has a practice in Brooklyn, and devotes most of his time to that, so he consistently has one of the worst absentee records in the assembly. Basically, he shows up only when the party needs his vote.'

'Do you have a picture?'

'No, I don't have any photos here, but he's as you described. Short and quite stout, and *very* sour in expression.' Cathman smiled faintly. 'He's a contrarian, which I think is the only reason he's come out against gambling. Of course, a number of the city legislators object because the city and Long Island have been excluded as gambling locations.'

'But he's known to be against gambling.'

'Oh, yes,' Cathman said. 'His name is on all such lists. He's spoken out against it, and he votes against it if he happens to be around.'

'You got a home address there?'

Again Cathman looked startled and worried. 'You're not going to— What are you going to do?'

'Look at him,' Parker said. 'Does he have letterhead stationery? Not as a lawyer, as an assemblyman.'

'Oh, yes, of course.'

'Get me some,' Parker said. 'And write down his address for me.'

Cathman dithered. He said, 'Nothing's going to . . . *happen* to him, will it? I mean, the man is . . . inoffensive, he's on our side, I wouldn't want . . .'

Slowly, Cathman ran down. He gazed pleadingly at Parker, who sat waiting for him. There was a notepad on the coffee table, and after a while Cathman pulled it close and copied the address.

13

Parker was the first to arrive. 'Lynch,' he said, and the girl in the black ball gown picked up three menus and the red leather-covered wine list and led him snaking through the mostly empty tables in the long dim room to the line of windows across the rear wall. Most of the lunchtime customers were clustered here, for the view. Parker sat with his left profile to the view, where he could still see the entrance, then looked out at what the other lunchgoers had come here to see.

First week in May. Sunlight danced on the broad river. Across the way, the Palisades made a vertical curtain of dark gray stone, behind which was New Jersey. This restaurant, called the Palisader and catering mostly to the tourist trade, was built on the eastern shore of the river, just above the city of Yonkers, New York City's neighbor to the north. That was the northeast corner of New Jersey over there, behind the Palisades, with New York State beginning just to the right, leading up toward West Point. A few sailboats roamed the river today, sunlight turning their white sails almost to porcelain. There were no big boats out

70

there.

Parker looked away from the view, and saw Mike Carlow come this way, following the same hostess. He nodded at Parker, took the seat across from him, then looked out at the view. 'Nothing yet, I guess,' he said.

'Not yet.' Cathman had said it would happen between one and three, and it was now just twelve-thirty.

'I've got a sister in Connecticut,' Carlow said. 'If we're gonna do this thing, I might bunk in with her for a while, save all this flying around.'

'Well, it's looking real,' Parker said, and the girl came swishing back through the tables, this time with huge Dan Wycza in her wake. She gestured toward Parker and Carlow with a slender hand and wrist that only emphasized Wycza's bulk, smiled at them all impersonally, and sailed away.

Wycza looked at the remaining places at the table; he could sit with his back to the view or to the door. 'Never be last,' he announced, and pulled out the view-facing chair. Settling carefully into it, the chair creaking beneath him, he said, 'So we'll do it?'

'Unless something new happens,' Parker told him. 'I called Lou Sternberg again this morning, he'll come over next week.'

'Good.' Wycza picked up his menu, but then looked out at the river and said, 'What we need's somebody that can walk on water.'

71

Carlow grunted. 'They don't play on our team,' he said.

Wycza shrugged. 'If the price is right,' he said, and studied the menu.

Their order was taken by a skinny boy wearing a big black bow tie that looked as though somebody was pulling a practical joke on him. After he left, Parker said, 'We need a woman. Not to walk on water.'

'What about yours?' Wycza asked him.

Parker shook his head, 'Not what she does.'

Carlow asked, 'What do we need?'

'Young, thin, good-looking. That could look frail maybe.'

Grinning, Wycza said, 'Like the little lady led me here.'

'Like that,' Parker agreed. 'But one of us.'

Carlow said, 'There was a girl with Tommy Carpenter like that. You know Tommy?'

'We worked on something together with Lou Sternberg once,' Parker said. 'What was her name? Noelle.'

'Noelle Braselle,' Carlow said, and smiled. 'I always thought that was a nifty name.'

Parker said, 'But she comes with Tommy, doesn't she? That's two more slices, not one.'

Shaking his head, Carlow said, 'Tommy got arrested or something. Well, they both did.'

'That's the job,' Parker said. 'The same job, with Lou. Some paintings we took. Those two got grabbed, but then they got let go, they had a good lawyer.'

72

'Well, it scared Tommy,' Carlow said. 'You wouldn't think he'd be a guy to spook, but he did. He quit, right then and there.'

Wycza said, 'Do I know these people?'

'I don't think so,' Parker said.

'You'd remember Noelle,' Carlow told him.

Parker said to Carlow, 'Where's Tommy?'

'Out of the country. Went to the Caribbean somewhere, doing something else. Nothing bent, he doesn't want the arm on him ever again. Left Noelle without a partner, but the last I heard, she's still around.'

Parker said, 'Can you find her? I'd have gone through Tommy's contact, but that can't be any good now.'

'I'll ask,' Carlow said.

Wycza said, 'I smell my money.'

They looked at him, and he was gazing out the window, and when they turned that way the ship was just sliding into view from the left. On the gleaming blue-gray water, among the few sailboats, against the dark gray drapery of the Palisades, it looked like any small cruise ship, white and sparkly, a big oval wedding cake, except in the wrong setting. It should be in the Caribbean, with Tommy Carpenter, not steaming up the Hudson River beside gray stone cliffs, north out of New York City.

'I can't read the name,' Carlow said. 'You suppose they changed it already? *Spirit of the Hudson*?'

'They changed that name,' Wycza assured

73

him, 'half an hour out of Biloxi.'

Parker looked at the ship, out in the center channel. A big shiny white empty box, going upriver to be filled with money. For the first time, he was absolutely sure they were going to do it. Seeing it out there, big and slow and unaware, he knew it belonged to him. He could almost walk over to it, on the water.

TWO

1

The same bums were in the Lido. Parker stood at the street end of the bar to have his beer, then went out to the gray day—no sunlight this time—to lean against the Subaru for two minutes until Hanzen came shuffling out of the bar and headed this way along the sidewalk. Then Parker wordlessly got behind the wheel, and Hanzen slid into the passenger seat beside him, and Parker drove on down Warren Street toward the invisible river.

Hanzen said, 'Where we going today?'

'Drive around and talk.'

'Take it out of town, then,' Hanzen advised. 'Do your left on Third Street.'

There were lights at every intersection, not staggered. When he could, Parker turned left on Third Street, and within a couple of blocks they were away from houses and traffic lights, with scrubby woodland on both sides of the road.

Hanzen, sounding amused, said, 'I guess you want me to go first.'

'If you got something to say,' Parker said.

'I talked to Pete Rudd about you.'

'I know you did.'

'And I know you know. Pete told me what you do, and I could trust you as long as you could trust me.'

'I don't trust your biker friends,' Parker said.

Hanzen snorted. 'I don't come attached to any bikers,' he said. 'I do business with those boys, that's all, and *I* wouldn't trust them around the corner.'

Parker said nothing to that. An intersection was coming up, with signs for a bridge across the river, and Hanzen said, 'Bear to the left, we'll stay on this side and go south along the river.'

Parker did so, and after a minute Hanzen said, 'I get the feeling you want *me* to tell *you* what your story is.'

'If you want.'

They were on a two-lane concrete road. There was woodsy hillslope up to their left, and the same down to their right, with the slate-gray river every once in a while visible down there. Nodding at the river, Hanzen said, 'There's only one change I know of lately, out there.'

'Uh huh.'

'It's got a boat full of money.'

'Uh huh.'

'And here you are.'

Parker said nothing to that, so Hanzen said, 'Pete probably told you I done time.'

'He didn't have to.'

76

'Well, yeah, I suppose he didn't. The thing is, I don't want to do any more.'

'Good,' Parker said.

Hanzen said, 'There's fellas, and you know them, too, that *like* to be in there. They won't admit it, they probably don't even know it themselves, but they like it. They like not having to be in charge of their own life, not having that chance to fuck up all the time. Life is regular, simple routines, food not so bad, you can pick some okay guys to be your pals, you don't have to be tense any more.'

Parker drove. Traffic was light, mostly pickup trucks and delivery vans. Hanzen said, 'You get into a little job with a fella like that, he's just waiting the chance to make that mistake, screw it up just enough so he can say, you got me, officer, and back into the nest he goes. And you with him.'

'They exist,' Parker agreed.

Hanzen said, 'I'm not one of them. I like it out here where I am. So if there's any chance at all, you and whoever you're in with, you're gonna come off that boat in chains, don't even tell me about it.'

'Then I'll drive you back to the Lido,' Parker told him, but didn't turn around. 'Because you ought to know there's *always* a chance something goes wrong. Pete must've told you, I done a number of things for a while now, and never wound up in chains. But every time, it could've happened.'

'Security's gonna be shit-tight on that boat.'

'Security's tight everywhere there's money.'

'That's true. You'd want me to take you out there, after dark, so you can board?'

'No, we'll get aboard our own way.'

'So it's when you're coming off. You and the money.'

'Right.'

'You coming down ropes? Won't they see you?'

'There's a door in the side of the ship, it's what they use themselves when they take the money off. It's five, six feet above the waterline, to be the right level for the dock. There's no windows next to it or under it.'

'You've got somebody giving you plans and things.'

Parker drove. They went through a little town with a gas station and a blinker light. Hanzen said, 'That wasn't a question.'

'I know.'

'Okay. It don't sound bad. I'm just there in the river, I'm minding my own business, here comes the boat. I see a fuss on that boat, I don't even come over. Don't look to me for no James Bond rescues.'

'I don't look to anybody for James Bond rescues,' Parker assured him.

'When you figure to do this?'

'You worried about the chains?'

'Not as long as I'm just some of the traffic out there in the river.'

'Then I'll call you,' Parker said. 'You won't need a lot of advance notice.'

Hanzen laughed. 'Trust is a wonderful thing,' he said.

2

'It isn't the lap of luxury,' the real estate agent said, 'but the price is right. And you fellas don't care about fancy stuff, I don't think.'

'Not us,' Mike Carlow agreed. 'We just like to come up from the city, weekends, do some fishing.'

'Then this is the place for you,' the real estate agent said. He was a jolly round-faced man with bushy white hair over his ears, so that he looked like a beardless Santa Claus. 'I'm a fisherman myself, you know,' he said.

'Oh, yeah?' Carlow actually looked interested. 'What do you go after, mostly?'

'Trout. Not in the Hudson, but in the little streams coming in.'

Carlow and the real estate agent continued through the house, talking crap about fishing, while Parker looked around, thinking it over. Was this the place for them?

It was just north of a small river town about thirty miles south of Albany, on the east side of the river, the same as Hanzen's mooring, but farther upstream. A dirt road led in from the state highway, past several rundown private houses, to this piece of land on a low bluff about fifteen feet above the water.

Four small cottages had been built here, back in the twenties, and hadn't been taken care of much since. They stood side by side in a row, identical rectangles facing away from the river, with shingle roofs and clapboard siding painted a worn green. They were shabbily old-fashioned, from their rattly and holey screen doors to the lines-and-squares pattern linoleum on their kitchen floors. There was room to park a car beside each, and a screened porch on the back of each one faced the river. Beyond them, at the end of a brief stone path, an old wooden staircase with a log railing led from the bluff down to a mooring and a short wooden pier.

These cottages were rented to vacationers, by the week or the month, but very few vacationers wanted to rough it with this sort of accommodation any more. The real estate agent had told the two of them frankly, driving them out here from his office on the highway, that only the occasional group of fishermen was likely to want to rent any of the cottages, and that at the moment none of them was occupied. 'The owners, a couple sisters, live away, one in Washington, DA, and the other over near Boston. They inherited, they don't much give a damn about the place, just so it pays the taxes and the insurance and the maintenance. Hunting season, especially deer season, they'll be rented out full, but the rest of the year they're mostly empty.'

There was nothing to choose between them; they were identical. Inside, there was a small living room with a fireplace and pine paneling and just enough furniture to get by, a very small kitchen with twenty-year-old appliances in it, a closet of a bathroom with appliances even older, and three small but neat bedrooms, each with a double bed, a dresser, an armoire, one bedside table, one bedside lamp, one ceiling light and no closet.

There was a number of such places up and down the river, left over from a time when upstate New York was a part of New York City's vacation land, before the jumbo jets opened the world. Most tourist accommodations around here had been torn down by now, replaced by housing or farming or light industry, but along the poorest parts of the river there had never been an economic reason to change, since nobody was going to come here anymore anyway.

This spot, Tooler's cottages, was the best location Parker and Mike Carlow had seen in the last three days of being two New Yorkers, working men, looking for a cheap place along the river for fishing weekends for themselves and their friends for the next month or so. No other houses were visible from here, and the cottages would be hard to notice from the river.

Coming out, they'd asked their usual question. Would the owner mind if other people were invited along sometimes? Not a bit. 'Long as you don't burn the place down,' the real estate agent told them, 'the Tooler sisters don't care what you do.'

He'd said, during their first conversation back in his little cluttered office with the Iroquois Indian memorabilia all over the place, that he had three houses he thought would suit them, but that the Tooler cottages were probably the best, so why didn't they take a look at them first? Fine. Now the question was, would there be any point looking at his other two possibles.

Parker and Carlow had seen almost two dozen rentals the last three days, and there'd been something wrong with every one of them. There were neighbors too close, or the access to the river wasn't simple enough, or the owner would be too inquisitive, or it was right next to a county road. This one had privacy, accessibility from both land and water, and absentee owners.

Parker met up with the other two in the living room, where Carlow was still talking fish. Maybe, when he wasn't driving cars, Carlow was a fisherman; he'd never said, and Parker had never asked.

Now, Carlow said, 'What do you think, Ed? Looks good to me.'

'Fine,' Parker said. He was being Edward Lynch again.

'And the price is right,' the real estate agent assured them, grinning at them both, happy to have some profit out of his morning's work.

Carlow said, 'And there's room, some of the other guys want to come up sometime, room for them, too.'

The real estate agent said, 'Just don't use more than one cottage, okay? The Toolers got a maid comes in once a week, cleans up, makes sure everything's okay. If she tells the Toolers there's two cottages been used, but I only show rent for one, there'll be hell to pay.'

'Then we'll only use the one,' Carlow promised.

Parker said, 'What day does she come?'

'Monday. People usually leave after a weekend, so Marie comes in on Mondays.'

Not a problem, then; they planned to do their thing on a Friday. Parker said, 'Anybody else come here?'

Carlow explained, 'Ed wants to know do we have to lock up,' which wasn't true, but a good thing to say.

The real estate agent grinned and shook his head. 'I don't think you *could* lock up,' he said, 'unless you brought your own, and your own hasps. I know there's fewer keys than doors, and there's at least two of these back doors, old wood, shrunk down, you can push 'em open when they're locked.'

Parker said, 'So nobody else comes around.'

'The propane gas man makes deliveries. If you boys take the place, I'll call him and tell him, and he'll come by with two fresh bottles. Otherwise, nobody else comes out.' Grinning again, he said, 'You won't get mail here.'

'Good,' Parker said, and Carlow said, 'That's what we want, get away from it all.'

'I knew this was the right place for you fellas,' the real estate agent said.

Parker said, 'I'll pay you the rent and deposit with a money order, if that's okay. Neither of us wants his wife to see this place in the checking account.'

The real estate agent laughed hugely. 'You boys got it all worked out,' he said.

'We hope so,' Carlow said.

3

'I'd vote for him,' Wycza said.

He and Parker stood in the international arrivals building of American Airlines at JFK, where the passengers from the London flight were just now coming through the wide doorway from Customs and Immigration. Waiting for them out here were some relatives, a lot of chauffeurs holding up signs with names written on them, and Parker and Wycza. Parker had just pointed out the guy they were waiting for, Lou Sternberg, the American heister who lived in London and who was going to be their state assemblyman.

Short and stout, with thick black hair and a round face wearing a habitual expression of grievance, Lou Sternberg was in a rumpled brown suit and open Burberry raincoat, and he walked with slow difficulty, twisted to one side to balance the heavy black garment bag that weighed down his right shoulder. A smaller brown leather bag dangled from his left hand. He looked like a businessman escaping a war zone, and pissed off about it.

'Travels light,' Wycza commented.

'He likes to be comfortable,' Parker said.

'Yeah? He don't look comfortable to me.'

Sternberg had seen them now, so Parker turned around and walked out, Wycza with him, and Sternberg trailing. They went out past the line of people waiting for taxis, and the inner roadway full of stopped cars at angles with their trunks open, and paused at the outer roadway, where Wycza pushed the traffic-light button.

Before the light changed to green, Sternberg caught up with them, huffing and red-faced. He was known for dressing too warmly for any climate he was in, so he was sweating now, rivulets down his round cheeks.

Parker said, 'Dan, Lou.'

Wycza nodded. 'How ya doin'.'

'Miserable,' Sternberg told him, looked him

up and down, and said, 'You look big enough to carry this bag.'

'So do you,' Wycza told him, but then shrugged and grinned and said, 'But what the hell.' He took the garment bag and put it on his own shoulder, and it seemed as though it must be much lighter now.

The light was green for pedestrians. They walked over into the parking lot and down the row toward the car Wycza was using, a large forest-green Lexus, big enough so Wycza could ride around in it without feeling cramped. Unlocking the Lexus, they put Sternberg's bags in the trunk and Sternberg in the back seat, where he sat and huffed like a long distance swimmer after a tough race.

Wycza drove, Parker beside him, and as they headed out of the airport Parker turned partway around in the seat to tell Sternberg, 'The guy you've got to look at is in Brooklyn, but there aren't any hotels in Brooklyn, so we're putting you in one in Manhattan, but way downtown, so it won't take you long to get over there.'

Sternberg had taken out a large white handkerchief and was mopping his face. He said, 'Who's financing?'

'We're doing it ourselves, as we go,' Parker told him. 'There isn't that much for the setup.'

'So I must be here legitimately,' Sternberg said. 'I know, I'm looking at art.'

'Then that's why you're downtown,' Parker

told him. 'Near the galleries.'

'I think of everything,' Sternberg agreed. Then he said, 'I don't know our driver here, Dan—thank you, Dan, for carrying that goddam heavy bag—but I take it he's a good friend of yours. Who else is aboard? Anyone I know?'

'Two you know,' Parker told him. 'Talking about art. Remember that painting heist went wrong?'

'Unfortunately, yes.'

'There was a girl in it, Noelle Braselle.'

'Oh, yes,' Sternberg said, brightening up. 'A tasty thing. Tommy Carpenter's girl, isn't she?'

'Was. He's off the bend, she's still on.'

'I liked looking at her, as I recall. So that's a plus. Who else?'

'Our driver's Mike Carlow, he says he worked with you in Iowa once, with Ed Mackey.'

'I do remember him,' Sternberg said. 'He came in at the last minute, something happened to the first driver, I forget what. He seemed all right. Anybody else?'

'I got a river rat to run the boat we need,' Parker told him. 'He isn't one of us, isn't a part of the job, he's just the guy with the boat. So we don't tell him a lot, don't hang out with him.'

'Where'd you get him?'

'A fella named Pete Rudd, that's reliable.'

'I don't think I know any Rudds, but I'll take

your word for it. Does this river rat get a full share?'

'No.'

Sternberg smiled. 'Does he get anything?'

Parker shrugged. 'Sure, why not. If he does his job, and lets it go at that.'

4

All-City Surgical and Homecare Supply occupied an old loft building in the east twenties of Manhattan, among importers, jobbers, restaurant equipment wholesalers, and a button manufacturer. Because there are petty thieves always at work in the city, every one of these buildings was protected at night by heavy metal gates over their street-level entrances and display windows, plus gates locked over every window that faced a fire escape.

Because none of the businesses on this block did much by way of walk-in trade, they all shut down by five or six in the afternoon, so when Parker and Carlow drove down the block at quarter after six that Wednesday evening nothing was open. One curb was lined with parked cars, but there was very little moving traffic and almost no pedestrians.

They stopped in front of All-City Surgical and Homecare, and got out of the van they'd lifted earlier today over in New Jersey. On both sides, the van said, TRI*STATE CARTAGE, with a colored painting of a forklift. Carlow stood watching as Parker bent over the padlock holding the gate and tried the half-dozen keys in his palm, one of which would have to work on this kind of lock.

It was the third. Parker removed the padlock, opened the hasp, and shoved the gate upward. It made a racket, but that didn't matter. It was full daylight, they were clearly workmen doing a legitimate job, they had a key, they weren't trying to hide or sneak around, and what would they find to steal, anyway, in a place full of wheelchairs and crutches?

The fourth of another set of keys opened the entrance door, and as they stepped inside Parker was already taking the small screwdriver from his pocket. Right there was the alarm keypad, just to the left of the door, its red light gleaming in the semi-darkness. While Carlow lowered the gate and shut the door, Parker unscrewed the pad and pulled it from the wall. He had either thirty or forty-five seconds, depending on the model, before the pad would signal the security company's office; plenty of time. He didn't know the four-digit code that would disarm the system, but it would work just as well to short it across these two connections back here.

Done. He put the pad back in the wall,

screwed it in place, and Carlow said, 'There's some over here.'

Wheelchairs.

It was a deep broad dark shop, with a counter facing forward near the back, and two doors in the wall beyond it leading to what must be storage areas. Here in the front part, there were shelves and bins down both sides, behind lines of wheelchairs, motorized and not, plus scooters for the handicapped and wooden barrels with forests of crutches standing in them.

Parker found a switch for the overhead fluorescents, turned it on, and they went over to see what was available. A lot of different kinds, it turned out, but what they wanted was a non-motorized wheelchair with handles that extended back so someone could push it. There were different kinds of those, too, so next they were interested in what was under the seat of each kind.

'Take a look at this,' Carlow said.

He'd found one with an enclosed black plastic box built in beneath the seat, curved across the front and angled where the sides met the back. There was a chrome handle in the middle of the back, and when Carlow had tugged on it the whole box slid back. It had no top except the seat, against which it made a tight fit, though the seat didn't move with the box, and the inside was filled almost completely by a white plastic bowl with an

90

arced metal rod attached to it. When stashed, the metal rod lay flat in a groove on top of the bowl, but when the box was pulled out the rod could be lifted into a carrying handle, and the bowl would lift out.

They looked at this thing. Carlow lifted the bowl out of the box and looked at the blank black space inside it, shaped to fit the bowl. He put the bowl back. Meantime, Parker looked at the seat and saw the cushion was a donut, with a hole in the center, and a round panel in the plastic seat itself could be swiveled out of the way, revealing a hole above the bowl. 'It's so whoever's in the wheelchair can go to the can,' he said. 'There's probably tubes and such, somewhere around here.'

'Jesus,' Carlow said. He pushed the box back under the seat, where it clicked into place. 'What a life,' he said.

'You'd get used to it,' Parker told him. 'People get used to everything but being dead.'

Carlow went on to look at other wheelchairs, but Parker stayed with the one with the bowl. He studied the way the parts were put together, the wheels and the frame and the seat and the back and the foot supports and the handles.

After a while, Carlow came over again. 'This one, you think?'

'Is there another one like it?'

'Yeah, same gray. Over there.'

'We'll take them both,' Parker said.

91

'What do we need two for?'

'Because I want the second box. If we walk out of here with two wheelchairs, no signs of entry, nothing fucked up, they'll think their records are wrong. And if they don't, the cops will. But if we take just the box and leave the chair, they'll *know* somebody was in here. I don't want a lot of cops looking for a hot wheelchair.'

'Okay.' Carlow gave the wheelchair a critical look. 'You sure that's big enough down there?'

'We can move the seat up, dick around with it a little. There'll be room.'

Carlow was still not sure, although Parker was already walking one of the wheelchairs toward the door. Carlow called after him, 'Won't they pull that handle? Won't they look in there?'

'Not twice,' Parker said over his shoulder, and Carlow laughed and went to get the other wheelchair.

5

Normally, Parker would stay as far as he could from any civilian that might be involved with a piece of work, and he'd prefer to stay away from Cathman, too, but he couldn't. The man bothered him, he rang tin somehow. Was he a nutcase all of a sudden, after all those years running in the squirrel cage, liking it? If so, what kind of nutcase was he, and how much trouble could he cause if he flipped out the rest of the way? And if not, if Cathman actually had some sort of idea or plan behind what he was doing, Parker needed to know that, too. No civilian agendas allowed.

According to Claire, Cathman had owned his home, a single-family house in an Albany suburb called Delmar, for twenty-seven years. Mortgage all paid up, his free and clear. His three daughters grew up there and married and moved out. His wife died there, seven years ago. He was still in the house. It ought to know everything about him by now.

Parker drove the Subaru down that block at three-thirty in the afternoon. Small two-story clapboard houses dating from the late forties' building boom lined both sides, each with a neat lawn in front and a neat driveway to one side. They'd started out looking all the same, cookie-cutter tract houses, but owners had altered and adapted and added to them over the years, so that by now they looked like relatives but not clones.

Cathman's was number 437, and his additions had been an attached garage at the top of the driveway and the enclosing of the front porch with windows that bounced back the spring sun. Shades were drawn over those windows and over the front windows upstairs.

Parker took the next left and drove two

blocks back out to the main shopping street, where there was a supermarket on the near right corner. He left the Subaru there, put on the dark blue jacket that read *Niagara-Mohawk Electric* across the back, picked up the clipboard from the passenger seat, and walked away down the sidewalk, the only pedestrian in miles.

In front of Cathman's house, he stopped to consult the clipboard, then walked up the driveway. A narrow concrete path went around the garage, and he followed it to the back yard, which was weedy and shaggy and uncared for. Chain-link fence separated it from the better-kept yards to both sides, and a tall wooden fence had been built for privacy by the neighbor at the rear. Some kids were playing with toy trucks in a yard half a block down to the right; they never glanced Parker's way.

The lock on the kitchen door was nothing. He went through it without damaging it, and spent the next hour tossing the house, careful but thorough. He moved furniture so he could roll up carpets to look for trapdoors to hiding places. He checked the ceilings and back walls of closets, and removed every drawer from every dresser and table and desk and built-in in the house. He stuck a knife in the coffee and in the flour, he took the backs off both TVs, he took off and then replaced every light switch and outlet plate. At the end, he put everything back the way it had been.

94

Nothing was hidden, nothing here changed the idea of Cathman as a solid citizen, predictable and dull. The only thing new Parker learned was that Cathman was looking for a job. He'd written more or less the same letter to about twenty government agencies and large corporations, listing his qualifications and stating his availability. The answers he got—and he always got an answer—were polite and respectful and not interested.

Clearly, he did this stuff at home, in this office upstairs at the back of the house that must originally have been a daughter's bedroom, because he didn't want his Rosemary Shields to know he was on a job hunt. That consulting business was just a face-saver, it cost him money instead of making money. He wasn't strapped yet, but how long could he keep up the fake show? Was that reason enough to turn to the heisters?

Parker finished with the house at ten to five. There was no beer in Cathman's refrigerator, but an open jug of Italian white wine was in there, cork stuck partway back in the bottle. Parker poured himself a glass, then sat in the dim living room and thought about the things that needed to be done. Noelle. The wheelchair. An ambulance or some kind of van that could take the wheelchair with a person in it. The limo for Lou. The chauffeur uniform. The guns. And Cathman's part: ID.

He heard the garage door motor switch on, and got up to go to the kitchen, where the side door connected with the garage. He refilled his glass, and poured a second, and when Cathman walked in, slope-shouldered and discouraged, Parker was just turning with a glass in each hand. 'You look like you could use this,' he said.

Cathman stared at him, first in astonishment, then in fear, and then, when he understood the glass that was extended toward him, in bewilderment. 'What—what are you—'

'Take the glass, Cathman.'

Cathman finally did, but didn't immediately drink. And now, because of having been startled and scared, he was moving toward anger. 'You broke in here? You just come in my *house*?'

'We'll talk in the living room,' Parker told him, and turned away, and Cathman had no choice but to follow.

The electric company jacket and the clipboard were on the sofa. Parker sat next to them, drank some wine, put the glass on the end table beside him, looked at Cathman standing in the doorway unable to figure out what to do next, and said, 'Sit down Cathman, we got things to talk about.'

Cathman blinked at him, and looked around the room. Trying to sound aggrieved, but coming off as merely weak, he said, 'Did you *search* in here?'

96

'Naturally.'

'Naturally? Why? What did you want to find?'

'You,' Parker said. 'You don't add up, and I want to know why.'

'I told you who I am.'

Parker said nothing to that. Cathman looked at the glass in his hand, as though just realizing it was there. He shook his head, walked over to sit in the easy chair to Parker's right, and drank a small sip from the glass.

Parker wanted to shake him up, disturb him, see what fell out, but at the same time not to spook him so much he couldn't be useful any more. So he'd come in here and show himself, but not make a mess. Not sit in the living room in the dimness when he comes home, but stand in the kitchen and offer him a glass of wine. Give a little, then get hard a little. Watch the reactions. Watch him, for instance, just take that tiny sip of wine and put the glass down. So he's under good control, whatever's driving him it isn't panic.

Cathman put the glass down, and frowned at Parker. 'Did you learn anything, coming in here like this?'

'You aren't a consultant, you're a guy out of work.'

'I'm both, as a matter of fact,' Cathman said. 'I know your type, you know. You want to be just a little menacing, so people won't try to take advantage of you, so they'll do what

97

you want them to do. But I don't believe it's just bluff, or I'd wash my hands of you now. It's habit, that's all, probably learned in prison. I'll do you the favor of ignoring it, and you'll do me the favor of not being more aggravating than you can help.'

'Well, you're pretty cool, aren't you?' Parker said. 'I came in here to read you, so now you're gonna read me.'

'I see you disguised yourself as a meter reader or some such thing,' Cathman said. 'But I'd rather you didn't do it again. If something goes wrong and you get arrested, I don't want to be connected to a criminal named Parker.'

Ignoring that, Parker said, 'What I need is ID, two pieces.'

Cathman frowned. 'What sort of ID?'

'You tell me. If an assemblyman is out on an official job of some kind, he might ask for bodyguards, right?'

'Not bodyguards, not exactly,' Cathman said. 'Oh, is that what you're going to do, go on board as assemblyman Kotkind? Is that why I gave you his letterhead stationery?'

'What do you mean, not exactly bodyguards?'

'He might ask for a state trooper, to drive him, if it's official.'

'In a patrol car?'

'No, a state car, with the state seal on the doors. Black, usually.'

'Trooper in uniform?'

98

'Probably not,' Cathman said. 'He'd be a plain-clothesman from the security detail.'

'Then that's the ID I want,' Parker said. 'Two of them.'

'They'd be photo IDs.'

'Then get me blanks. Get me something I can adapt.' Cathman picked up the wine glass, took a sip, brooded at Parker. He said, 'When are you going to do it? The robbery—'

'Pretty soon. So get me the IDs.'

'No, I mean *when*.'

'I know what you mean,' Parker told him. Leaving his wine unfinished, he got to his feet and said, 'I'll call you here, next Monday, in the evening, tell you where to bring them.'

Cathman also stood. 'Are you going to do it next week?'

Parker shrugged into the jacket, picked up the clipboard. 'I'll call you Monday,' he said, and left.

6

'I bet that's her,' Carlow said.

Parker looked, and it was. Among the people getting off the Chicago Trailways bus here at the Albany terminal, that was the remembered face and figure of Noelle Braselle. She looked to be about thirty, tall and slender and very together, but she also looked like a college girl, with her narrow-legged blue jeans and bulky orange sweater crossed by the straps of a dark blue backpack, and her straight brown hair pulled back from her oval face to a black barrette and a short ponytail. She saw Parker and Carlow across the street from the terminal and waved, and as the other disembarking passengers crowded around the driver while he pulled their luggage out from the bus's lower storage area, she came across to them, smiling. Noelle traveled light. 'Long time no see,' she said to Parker.

'You haven't changed,' he told her.

'I sure hope not,' she said, and raised a curious eyebrow at Carlow.

Parker said, 'Noelle, this is Mike Carlow. He's your driver.'

'My driver?'

'We're taking different routes, on the night. Come on, I'll tell you about it.'

They'd borrowed Wycza's big Lexus, for comfort, because it was almost an hour drive from here to Tooler's cottages, and it was parked now a block from the terminal. As they walked, Noelle said, 'You still got that nice lady stashed?'

'Claire,' Parker agreed. 'Yeah, we're together.'

'Good. Tommy and I split, you know.'

'I heard.'

'Funny,' she said. 'I used to think there wasn't anything would scare him, then all at

100

once everything did, and goodbye, Harry. Is this it? Nicer than a bus.'

'Very like a bus,' Carlow told her.

Carlow drove, Noelle beside him, Parker in back. They had to cross the river on one of the big swooping bridges here, and then head south. Parker said, 'You remember Lou Sternberg.'

'From that painting disaster? Angry guy, overweight, drove the big truck.'

'That's him. He's with us on this. And a guy I don't think you know, Dan Wycza.'

She turned to grin at Parker in the back seat and said, 'I hope this one comes out a little better.'

'It will,' he said.

*   *   *

Wycza, in shorts and sneakers, was doing push-ups on the weedy grass in the sun in front of the cottage. Noelle, seeing him as they drove in, laughed and said, 'Is this supposed to be my birthday?'

'Dan Wycza,' Parker told her, and Carlow said, 'For the heavy lifting.'

'I can see that,' she said. 'Is Lou Sternberg here?'

'Not yet. He's in Brooklyn, watching a guy for later.'

Wycza got to his feet when he saw the car coming. He offered a small wave and went into the house, while Carlow parked the Lexus. They got out, Noelle carrying her backpack slung over one shoulder, and went into the house, where Wycza stood now in the living room, rubbing his head and neck with a tan towel.

Parker said, 'Noelle Braselle, Dan Wycza.'

'Hi,' Wycza said, and Noelle frowned at him and said, 'I know you. Don't I know you?'

Grinning, Wycza said, 'I wish you did, honey.'

'No, I've seen you somewhere,' she said. The two wheelchairs were in this room, one still together, the other mostly apart; she hadn't remarked on them yet, but she did put her backpack on the complete one now as she continued to frown at Wycza, trying to place him.

'If I'd ever met you,' Wycza promised her, 'I'd remember. Trust me.'

All at once her brow cleared: 'You're a wrestler! That's where I saw you!'

Wycza gazed at her like he couldn't believe it. 'You're a fan?'

'I went with a guy a few times,' she said. 'I kind of loved it.'

Speaking confidentially, he said, 'It's all fake, you know. I'm not really getting beat up by those clowns.'

'I know! That's what's so great about it! I look at you, and I see you could open those guys like pistachios, and you just goof around

102

instead. Wait. Strongarm! You're Jack Strongarm.'

'Miss Braselle,' Wycza said, 'you got a convert.'

'Well, if that isn't something else,' she said, and shook her head at Wycza, and grinned. 'Nice to meet you.'

'And you. Believe me.'

She turned to Parker to say, 'You were gonna show me what I'm doing. Or should I get rid of my pack first? Which room is mine? What's with the wheelchair?'

'You're gonna be in it,' Parker told her.

'I am?'

'Every night, starting tomorrow, after we get you the right clothes, Mike's gonna be in his chauffeur suit, pushing you in the wheelchair, and you're gonna be the brave but broken debutante. You'll be six hours on the ship, Albany to Albany. You'll gamble a little, you'll watch a little, you'll do little brave smiles here and there.'

'Jesus, I despise myself,' she said. 'What am I playing this poor little rich girl for?'

Parker slid open the box under the seat, with the white plastic bowl in it. 'See this?'

'Oh,' she said. 'Don't tell me, let me guess.'

'This is a wheelchair for people who don't get out of it for anything.'

'I get the concept,' she said.

'Security's tight on that ship,' Parker told her. 'When you board, they'll look in there.'

'So what?'

'It won't be empty. You'll see to that.'

She made a disgusted face and said, 'Parker, what are you doing to me? That's going to be under me all night?'

'Six hours. It's airtight, no smell, nothing. But they'll look in it when you come aboard, and they may look in it when you go ashore. And they may the next night, and they may the night after that.'

She began to smile. 'And one of these nights they won't,' she said, 'because they know what's in there.'

'That's right.'

'So that's how the guns get on.'

'No,' he said, 'we're getting them on another way, that's what Lou's working on now. What you're doing is, you're taking the cash off.'

She looked around, and pointed, and said, 'That's what the other wheelchair's for.'

Wycza said, 'We're adapting it a little, the seat on that one's gonna be higher, so that night you hunker down some.'

'I can do that,' she said. She looked around at the three men and the two wheelchairs and the old-fashioned cottage and said, 'A new experience. I never hatched money before.'

7

Parker rode the *Spirit of the Hudson* just once before the night. Since, when it all went down, he'd be in disguise, this time he went open, alone, in jacket and tie. He bought some chips, and he noticed that most of the other people buying chips were using hundred-dollar bills. That was a good sign.

Because this was a new operation, nobody knew yet what the take would be. The ship was medium to small, holding just over eight hundred paying passengers, and if they on average dropped a hundred dollars apiece, including the twelve-dollar fare to come aboard, that would mean eighty thousand dollars in the money room by the end of the night. If the average loss was five hundred dollars, which some area newspapers had estimated, that would be four hundred thousand waiting for them. It was an acceptable range, and from what Parker was seeing, the result would most likely be toward the higher end.

It wasn't true that no credit cards at all were in use on the *Spirit of the Hudson*. Chips you could only buy with cash, but you could pay for your dinner or souvenirs with credit cards. The little bit of cash that came in from those sources didn't go to the casino money room, so

Parker didn't think about it.

The casino ship took two runs a day, from noon till six P.M. and from eight P.M. till two in the morning. Every trip began and ended in Albany, with one midway stop at Poughkeepsie, where a few passengers would board or depart and more supplies would be taken on. The money only left the ship, though, at Albany.

Parker chose a Friday night trip, the same as the night they'd be taking it down, to get a feel for the place. The ship was full, action in the casino was heavy, and the people having dinner in the glass-walled dining rooms to both sides of the casino as it sailed past the little river towns were dressed up and making an occasion of it. The sense was, and it was palpable through the ship, this was a fun way to spend money. Good.

From time to time, Parker saw Carlow and Noelle in the distance, but made sure to steer clear of them. Noelle, with a little pale makeup and dark gray filmy clothing that made her seem even more slender than she was, looked mostly like a vampire's victim. Carlow, pushing the wheelchair in his dark blue chauffeur's uniform and cap, leaning on the handles when it was at rest, looked wiry and tough, as though he were as much bodyguard as chauffeur.

People smiled at Noelle, who smiled wanly back. People touched her for luck, or asked her to blow on their dice, and whenever she played a little blackjack or shot craps for a while she was surrounded by people cheering her on.

Noelle and Carlow had been at this game for four nights now, and the security people still looked in the bowl every night—coming aboard, not going ashore—but Noelle was making sure they had a good variety to look at and they were beginning to get embarrassed, and also to recognize her, and to ease up. Parker figured by the middle of next week they'd just be waving her aboard.

He had studied the space and blueprints of the *Spirit of the Hudson*, and knew the ship well, at least in theory, but reality is never exactly the same as the space. He wandered the ship, getting to understand it in this new way, covering every part of it that was open to the passengers.

There were three public decks. The top one was all open promenade, a long oval around the bridge with a lot of deck chairs that probably got more action on the daytime run. The deck below that was wider, another promenade, this one glassed-in, because upstate New York doesn't get that much good weather year-round. This public oval surrounded an interior space of offices, a gift shop, a massage room, a game room with pinball machines, and a tiny joke of a library. The lifeboats were suspended just outside and below this promenade, not to spoil the view;

if anybody ever had to actually board those lifeboats, the glass panels in front of them could be slid out of the way.

The third deck down was the important one, the casino, taking up the entire interior of the ship, with no windows, and no doors that opened directly to the outside. It could be reached only through vestibules fore and aft. Everywhere on the ship you were always aware of the humming vibration of the engines and the thrust of them through the water, but in the casino you could very quickly forget that you were afloat.

Flanking the casino were two dining rooms, of different types. The one on the port side was more upscale, with cloth napkins and expensive entrees and an eight-page wine list, while the one to starboard was a sandwich joint. Both were long and narrow, their outer walls all glass. Both, Parker knew from the specs, were served by the same kitchen, directly below the casino, with escalators for the waiters to bring the platters up. And in the center of that kitchen was a round metal post, inside which were the pneumatic tubes that moved money; upward to the casino cashier, in the middle of the casino, in an elaborate cage, and downward to the money room.

There was one bit of public access below the casino; restrooms, fore and aft. Broad carpeted staircases led down from both vestibules outside the casino, to wide hushed low ceilinged areas that looked like hotel lobbies, scattered with low sofas and armchairs, with the men's and women's rooms off that.

In the aft lobby, near the stairs, an unmarked and locked door led to a simpler staircase that went down to the corridor that led to the money room. A guard would be on duty, at all times, the other side of that door, to keep people from coming in. He wouldn't worry, until too late, about keeping people from coming out.

The aft section also contained a small elevator from casino vestibule down to restroom lobby, for people who'd have trouble with the stairs. Once every evening, Noelle and Carlow would take that elevator down and, while Noelle waited outside, Carlow would take the bowl into the men's room and tip the attendant there very well to clean it out.

In the course of the evening, Parker ate small meals in both restaurants, when he could get tables. He also walked the glassed-in promenade, and the top deck open-air promenade, where he was completely alone. Although the ship produced a lot of light, with a creamy nimbus around it on the disturbed water, it was very hard to see in close at the side of the ship. From above, the view was outward, not down. If Hanzen came up from behind, and stayed close to the flank as he approached the open door, no one would see him.

When the ship docked at Albany at two in the morning, Parker was among the first off. He stepped back on the pier, out of the way of the others debarking, and watched that door open in the side of the hull. An armored car was already parked there, facing away from the ship, and once that doorway gaped black the armored car backed up to it until it was snug against the metal side of the ship.

Parker watched Noelle and Carlow go by, both looking solemn, as though what they'd just come out of was church. Neither looked in his direction, but Noelle waggled two fingers as they went by. She was having fun.

8

The man who had the guns was named Fox. *Maurice Fox*, it said on the window of the store, *Plumbing Equipment*, on a backwater side street in the former downtown of New Brunswick, New Jersey. This wasn't the kind of business to move out to the mall with all his former neighbors, so here he stayed, now with a storefront revivalist church on one side and a candle-and-incense shop on the other.

Parker left the Subaru in the loading zone in front of the store and went from the sunny outside to the dim interior, where the store

110

was long and narrow and dark. Dusty toilets were lined up in one row, porcelain sinks in another, and bins full of pipejoints and faucets lined one wall.

A short balding man in a rumpled gray suit and bent eyeglasses came down the aisle between the rows of toilets and sinks. 'Yes? Oh, Mr Flynn, I didn't recognize you, it's been a while.'

'I phoned you.'

'Yes, sure, of course. You don't go through Mr Lawson anymore.' James Lawson was a private detective in Jersey City who fronted for people like Fox, on the bend.

Parker said, 'Why should I? We already know each other.'

With a sad smile, Fox said, 'Cut out the middleman, that's what everybody does. In my business, most of the time, *I'm* the middleman, why should I love this philosophy? I think I got what you want, come look.'

There was a way to talk to this man on the telephone about plumbing equipment and wind up with guns, but when you have to be so careful about listening ears, sometimes it's hard to get the exact details right. But, as Fox turned away to lead Parker deeper into the store, he said, 'What I heard, you want two revolvers, concealment weapons such as plainclothes police might carry, and the shoulder holsters to go with them.'

'That's right.'

At the back of the shop, Fox led them through a doorway, which he shut behind them, and down a flight of stairs with just steps and no risers to a plaster-walled basement. At the bottom, Fox clicked a light switch on a beam, and to the left a bare bulb came on.

Now he led the way across the concrete floor, mounds of supplies in the darkness around them, to a wooden partition with a heavy wooden door. He took a ring full of keys from his pocket, chose one, and unlocked the door. They went inside, and Fox hit another light switch that turned on another bare bulb dangling from the ceiling. He closed this door, too, when they were inside.

The room was small and made smaller by the cases lining it on all four sides. The floor was wooden slats over concrete, except for one two-foot square in the middle, where there was no wood over the drain. Along the back wall the crates were crowded together on to wooden shelves, and Fox went directly over to them and took out a white cardboard box. The label pasted on the end claimed, with an illustration, that the box contained a bathroom sink faucet set.

A square dark table, paint-stained, stood in one corner. Fox carried the cardboard box to it, opened it, and inside, nestled in white tissue paper, was a nickel-plated .357 Magnum revolver, the S&W Model 27. This was the kind of gun developed for the police back in the thirties, when the mobsters first took to wearing body armor and driving around in cars with bulletproof glass, making the normal .38 almost useless. The .357 Magnum had so much more power it could go through a car from the rear and still have enough strength to kill the driver. One .357 slug could put out a car engine.

While Parker looked it over, Fox went away to his shelves and came back this time with a box claiming to contain a toilet float-ball; inside was another S&W 27. 'And holsters, one minute,' he said, and went away again.

When he came back, with two cartons of 'icemaker tubing', Parker held up the second of the revolvers and said, 'The serial number's off this one. Acid, looks like.'

Fox looked faintly surprised. 'Isn't that better?'

'It's got to be shown like a lawman would show it, hand it over and take it back. Maybe they're sharp-eyed, maybe they're not.'

'Ah. A problem.' Fox brooded at his wall of boxes. 'For the same reason,' he said, 'you'd probably like them both the same.'

'That would be good.'

'I got an almost,' Fox decided. 'The Colt Python. Looks the same, same size, same caliber. Could you use that?'

'Let me see it.'

Another bathroom sink set. The Python was as Fox had described, and looked a close relative of the 27. 'I'll take it,' Parker decided.

'You'll want to check them?'

Parker knew how that worked with Fox. Under the drain plate in the middle of the room was loose dirt. To test-fire Fox's merchandise, you stood above the drain and shot a bullet into the dirt. It made a hell of a racket here in this enclosed room, but Fox claimed the boxes absorbed all that noise and none of it was heard outside.

There were times when you expected to use a gun, and then you'd try it first, but this time, with what they planned on the ship, if they had to use one of these guns, the situation would already be a mess. The revolvers were both clean and well oiled, with crisp-feeling mechanisms; let it go at that. 'No need,' Parker said. 'I'll take them as they are. Let me see the holsters.'

They were identical, stiff leather holsters without a strap across the chest. They fit the 27 and the Python, and they were comfortable to wear. 'Fine,' Parker said.

'The whole thing is three hundred,' Fox said, 'and when you're done with them, if they haven't been used, you know, you understand what I mean—'

'Yes.'

'Well, we done business before,' Fox said. 'So, if you just use them for show, afterwards I'll be happy to buy them back at half price.'

Afterwards, no matter what happened,

114

these guns would be at the bottom of the Hudson. 'I'll think about it,' Parker said.

9

CONTINENTAL PATRIOT PRINTING said the old-fashioned shield-shaped sign hanging over the entry door. The shop was one of several in a long one-story fake-Colonial commercial building in a faded suburb of Pittsburgh, built not long after the Second World War and long since overwhelmed by the more modern malls. A few of the shops were vacant and for rent, and several of the remainder continued the Colonial theme: Paul Revere Video Rental down at the corner, Valley Forge Pizza next to the print shop.

The plate-glass display window of the print shop was crammed with multicolored posters describing the services available within: 'Wedding Invitations—Business Cards—Yearbooks—Letterheads—Newsletters—Announcements.' The one thing not mentioned was the service that had brought Parker here.

There was angled parking in front of the shops. Parker left the Subaru in front of Valley Forge Pizza and went into Continental Patriot Printing, where a bell rang when he opened the door, and rang again when he shut it.

The interior of this shop had been truncated, cut to a stub of a room by a hastily constructed cheap panel wall with an unpainted hollow-core door in it. The remaining space was divided by a chest-high counter facing the front door, again quickly made, and with cheap materials. The paneling across the front of the counter and the paneling of the partition itself were heavy with more posters promoting the services available here, with examples of the work that could be done. The general air was of a competent craftsman with too few customers.

The inner door opened, in response to that double bell, and an Asian man came out, in work shirt and jeans and black apron. He was around forty years of age, short and narrow-shouldered, with a heavy, forward-thrusting head, and eyes that squinted with deep suspicion and skepticism through round glasses. His name, Parker knew, was Kim Toe Kwai, and he was Korean.

He and Parker met at the counter, where Kim said, 'Yes? May I help you?' But beneath that professional courtesy was an undisguisable skepticism, the belief that this new person could not possibly help because nobody could.

'A fellow named Pete Rudd told me I should get in touch with you,' Parker said.

The suspicious eyes grew narrower, the mouth became a slit. 'I do not know such a man,' he said.

'That's okay,' Parker told him. 'I'll tell you what I need, and after I leave you can look in your address book or wherever and see do you know a Pete Rudd and call him and ask him if you should do business with Mr Lynch. You see what I mean?'

Kim took an order form out from under the counter and picked up a pen held there with a piece of cord tied around it and thumbtacked to the counter. He wrote 'Lynch' on the order form. He said, 'You have brochures you want made?'

'That's right,' Parker said, and while Kim wrote 'brochures' on the order form Parker took a laminated card out of his pocket, plus two small headshot photos, one of himself and the other of Wycza. The laminated card was a legitimate identification card for a New York State trooper. Putting it on the counter for Kim to see, but holding one finger on it, Parker said, 'At the end, I need the original back. Undamaged.'

Kim squinted at the ID, then frowned at Parker. 'This is actual,' he said.

'That's right. That's why I got to get it back.'

This was what Cathman had come up with, out of the state files; a solidly legitimate ID taken from a trooper currently on suspension for charges involving faked evidence against defendants. Whether the trooper was exonerated or not, Cathman needed to be able to put that ID back in the files, and soon.

Kim pointed at the photo of Parker and then at the ID. 'You want this,' he said, and then pointed at the photo of Wycza and again at the ID, 'and this.'

'Right.'

Kim wrote some scribbles on the order form, and then, in the right-hand charge column, he wrote, '$500 each.'

Parker put his hand palm down on the form. When Kim looked at him, waiting, Parker took the pen from him, and with the form upside down, he crossed out 'each.' Putting the pen down, reaching for his wallet, he said, 'Pete told me your price structure, and said you were fair in your charges.'

Kim gave a sour look, and a shrug. 'No doubt,' he said, as Parker slid five one-hundred-dollar bills from his wallet and put them on the counter, 'he also told you I do very fast work.'

'You're right, he did.'

'This is complex, this brochure.' Kim thought about it. 'Three days.'

'Thursday. I'll be here Thursday afternoon.'

'I close at five.'

'I'll be here,' Parker said.

Kim peeled off one copy of the order form and pushed it across the counter toward Parker, but Parker shook his head, not taking it. 'We'll remember each other,' he said.

118

10

On Assemblyman Morton Kotkind's letterhead stationery, Lou Sternberg addressed Andrew Hamilton, New York State Gaming Commissioner, and wrote as follows:

As you know, I have been opposed to the further legalization of gambling in New York State, beyond the lottery and the bingo for tax-exempts already existing. I have been in particular opposition to the installation of a gambling ship on the Hudson River, worldwide symbol of the Empire State, site of the first inland European exploration, by famed Henry Hudson in his ship the *Half Moon*, of what was to become the United States of America.

The will of the people's representatives, at this time, has seen fit to look the other way at the potential for abuse in this introduction of casino gambling into the very heart of our state, where our children can actually stand on the riverbank and see this floating casino, and judge thereby that such activity has the blessing of their elders.

Other esteemed members of the Assembly have assured me that the operation of this floating casino is utterly reputable, that the potential for corruption has been minimized, and that the anticipated tax revenues and economic benefits to the depressed areas of the Hudson River Valley far outweigh any potential for mischief or malfeasance. I am far from changing my attitude in this matter, but even my most severest critics have always had to acknowledge my open-mindedness. I am prepared to listen and to observe.

In this regard, I have decided to undertake a fact-finding tour of inspection of the floating casino on Friday, May 23, this year, on the eight P.M. sailing from Albany. I wish this mission to be as low-key as possible, with no excess attention paid to me and my two aides who will accompany me. I would ask merely for one escort from the ship's complement to conduct me on my tour. I will expect, of course, to see every part of the ship.

At this point, I would take strong exception to this tour of inspection being used for publicity purposes to suggest that my opposition to casino gambling in New York State has altered or diminished in any way. I shall myself make no contact with the press, and I would ask that your office and the operators of the floating casino do not alert the press to this tour of inspection. After the event, if you wish, we may make a joint public announcement.

My assistant, Dianne Weatherwax, will telephone your office from my constituent office in my district in Brooklyn on Wednesday, May 21, to finalize the details. Any questions you may have should be raised through her, at that office.

May I say that, although I do not expect to have my opinions on this issue changed, I would welcome convincing evidence that casino gambling is not the scourge I have long believed it to be.

Yours sincerely,
Morton Kotkind

Sternberg was proud of this letter. 'It sounds like him,' he said. 'Some of it is even from his speeches, like the children on the riverbank. And besides that, it's the way he talks.'

It had been part of Sternberg's job to meet Kotkind, study him, get to know him, befriend him. There was a bar near Kotkind's Brooklyn law offices on Court Street where lawyers went to unwind after their hard days, and it had not been difficult for Sternberg, short and stout and sour-looking, to blend in among them, cull Kotkind from the herd, and share a scotch and soda with the man from time to time.

And now Sternberg was upstate, at Tooler's cottages, with the letter. Parker and Wycza and Noelle and Carlow all read it, and all agreed it sounded like a politician/lawyer starting to reposition himself from off that limb he'd climbed out on.

Giving the letter back, Parker said to Sternberg, 'So you'll meet up with him on Tuesday—'

'We already got an appointment,' Sternberg said. 'We're both gonna be in court that day, him in state civil, me in housing, and we're gonna meet at the bar at five o'clock, have a drink before we go home to the trouble and strife, share our woes with the judges. That's when I slip him the mickey.'

'What I want is him sick,' Parker said. 'Through Saturday. Sick enough so he doesn't go to any office, make any phone calls, put in any appearances anywhere. But not so sick he gets into the newspapers. Assemblyman down with Legionnaires' disease; I don't need that.'

'I'll put him down,' Sternberg said, grinning, 'as gentle as a soft-boiled egg.'

The letter was dated Monday, May 12th, but wouldn't actually be mailed, in Brooklyn, until Friday the 16th, so it wouldn't get to Commissioner Hamilton's office until Monday the 19th at the earliest, four days before the tour of inspection. The Post Office would be blamed for the delay, and no one would think any more about it.

Kotkind's Brooklyn constituent office was a storefront open only on Mondays and Thursdays. Carlow and Sternberg had already invaded it twice without leaving traces, and knew how the office worked. Noelle would go to Brooklyn with them on Wednesday, and from the constituent office she'd phone Commissioner Hamilton to work out the details of Assemblyman Kotkind's visit, and she'd be happy to stick around a while so they could call her back, if for any reason they had to.

Parker said to Noelle, 'That's his administrative assistant, for real, Dianne Weatherwax, from Brooklyn, graduated from Columbia University in New York. Can you do her?'

'Shoe-uh,' said Noelle.

11

Throughout America, the states were settled by farmers, who mistrusted cities. State after state, when it came time to choose a spot for the capital, it was, put somewhere, anywhere, other than that state's largest city. From sea to shining sea, with the occasional rare exception like Boston in Massachusetts, the same impulse held good. In California, the capital is in Sacramento. In Pennsylvania, the capital is

Harrisburg; in Illinois it's Springfield; in Texas it's Austin. And in New York State, the capital is Albany.

State capitals breed buildings, office buildings, bars, hotels and restaurants, but they also breed parking lots. State-owned automobiles, somber gray and black, usually American-made, utterly characterless except for the round gold state seal on their doors, wait in obedient rows on blacktop rectangles all over Albany, each enclosed in a chain-link fence with a locked gate.

At seven-fifteen on an evening in May, in daylight, under partly cloudy skies with a slight chill in the air, Parker and Wycza stepped up to the chain-link gate in the chain-link fence surrounding the State Labor Department motor pool parking lot on Washington Street. Both wore dark suits, white shirts, narrow black ties. Wycza stood casually watching while Parker quickly tried the keys he held in the palm of his right hand. The third one snapped open the padlock and released the hasp.

While Wycza stood beside the open gate, Parker walked down the row of Chevrolets, his right hand dropping that first set of keys into his trouser pocket while his left hand brought out another little cluster of keys from his outside suitcoat pocket. Switching these to his right hand, he stopped next to one of the cars, tried the keys, and again it was the third one that did it.

The same key started the ignition. Parker drove the black car out of the lot and paused at the curb while Wycza locked the gate and got into the passenger seat, where he scrunched around and pulled his door shut and said, 'Couldn't you find anything bigger?'

'They're all the same,' Parker told him, and drove off, headed downtown.

As they drove, Wycza took the small bomb from his suitcoat pocket, set it for one forty-five A.M., and put it in the glove compartment. There'd be no way to remove all the fingerprints from this car, so the only thing to do was remove the car.

On State Street, they pulled over to stop in front of a bar with a wood shingle façade. Almost immediately, Lou Sternberg, in a pinstripe dark blue suit and pale blue shirt and red figured tie, came out of the place, briskly crossed the sidewalk and got into the back seat. 'I was hoping for a limo,' he said.

Wycza said, 'You're only an assemblyman.'

Parker steered back into traffic, heading downtown and downhill, toward the river.

The *Spirit of the Hudson* had its own parking area, on the landward side of an old converted warehouse, which until the gambling ship arrived had been empty for several years. Now a part of its ground floor had been tricked up with bright paint and plastic partitions and flying streamers and pretty girls in straw hats, and this is where the customers were processed, where they paid for their tickets and signed their waivers to absolve the operators of the ship from any kind of liability for any imaginable eventuality, and received their small shopping bag of giveaways: a pamphlet describing the rules of the games of chance offered aboard, a map of the segment of the *Hudson* they'd be traveling, pins and baseball caps with the ship's logo, and a slip of paper warning that chips for the games could only be bought with United States currency; no credit cards.

Parker and Wycza and Sternberg ignored that normal way in. At the far end of the warehouse, a blacktop road led around toward the pier, where supplies would come aboard. Parker steered around that way, and when he got to the guard's kiosk he opened his window and said, 'Assemblyman Kotkind.'

'Oh, yes, sir!' The word had gone out, treat this politico well, we may have a convert. Stooping low to smile in at Sternberg in the back seat, the guard said, 'Evening, Mister Assemblyman.' Then, to Parker, he said, 'Just go on down there and around to the right. There's a place for you to park right down there where the people get aboard.

'Thank you,' Parker said, and drove on.

A pretty girl with a straw hat and a clipboard saw them coming, and trotted briskly over to meet them, smiling hard. Looking in at Parker, she said, 'Is this the assemblyman?'

126

'In the back,' Parker told her. 'Do I leave the car here?'

'Oh, yes, fine. No one will disturb it.'

Well, that wasn't exactly true. Parker and Wycza got out on their own, but the girl opened the rear door for Sternberg, who came out scowling and said, 'Are you my escort?'

'Oh, no, sir,' she said. 'Someone on the ship will see to you. If you'll just—'

'I'd rather,' Sternberg said, because it seemed like a good idea to be difficult from the very beginning, 'meet the person here, be escorted aboard.'

'Oh, well, yes, fine,' she said, her smile as strong as ever. Pulling a walkie-talkie from a holster on her right hip, she said, 'Just let me phone up to the ship.'

While she murmured into the walkie-talkie, Parker and Wycza and Sternberg looked over at the stream of passengers coming out of the warehouse and passing along the aisle flanked by red-white-and-blue sawhorses to the short ramp to the ship, that ramp being covered by red-white-and-blue canvas tarp walls and roof. The people seemed happy, cheerful, expectant. It was twenty to eight, and there were already a lot of customers visible moving around on the ship. Friday night; the *Spirit of the Hudson* was going to be full.

'Look at that poor child in the wheelchair,' Sternberg said. 'And gambling.'

'Oh, yes, sir,' the girl said, determinedly

127

sunny. 'She comes every night. It seems to cheer her up. Ms Cahill will be down in a moment. Oh, I see her coming.'

They all did, emerging from the tarp-covered ramp, a tall slim woman, attractive but more substantial than the girls in the straw hats, she in low-heeled pumps, dark blue skirt and jacket, white ruffled blouse. When she approached their group, her smile looked metallic, something stamped out of sheet tin. The hand she extended, with its long coral-colored nails, seemed made of plastic, not flesh. 'Mister Assemblyman,' she said, as though delighted to meet him. 'I'm Susan Cahill, I talked with your Dianne Weatherwax on Wednesday.'

'Yes, she mentioned you,' Sternberg said, grumpily, accepting her hand as though it was only the likelihood that she was a voter that made him do it. 'This is my escort, Mr Helsing and Mr Renfield.' Parker had not given Kim Toe Kwai any specific names to use on the IDs he'd made up, and he'd apparently been watching a Dracula movie recently.

Susan Cahill turned to offer a lesser smile to these lesser beings, and Parker said, 'My identification,' showing her Kim's first-rate handiwork in its own leather ID case, explaining, 'Mr Renfield and I are both carrying firearms. One handgun each. I'm required to tell you that before we embark, and to explain, the law forbids us to give up the weapons when we're on duty.'

She blanched a bit, but said, 'Of course, I understand completely. If I may?'

He held the ID case open so she could read. She was brisk about it, then nodded and said, 'Thank you for informing me.'

'We'll have to inform the captain, too.'

'I'll take care of that,' she assured him.

Wycza had his own ID case out. 'This is mine,' he said, but as he extended it she said, 'No, I'm sure everything's fine. Mister Assemblyman, would you and your escort follow me?'

'Before we go,' Sternberg said, 'I want to make one thing perfectly clear. This is not an official visit. I am on a fact-finding mission only. I shall not be gambling, and I shall not want any special treatment, merely a conducted tour of the ship.'

'And that's what you'll get, Mister Kotkind,' Susan Cahill assured him. 'Gentlemen?'

They cut the line of boarding passengers, but no one minded. People could tell they were important.

THREE

1

Ray Becker waited an hour after they'd left, the man called Parker and the big one, both in dark suits and ties, the girl in her wheelchair that she didn't need, driven in the Windstar van by the guy in the chauffeur suit, all of them off and away on a Friday night, a big night in the world of casinos, all dressed up to put on a show. Tonight's the night. It's over at last.

Five after six they'd driven away in the two vehicles, the Subaru and the van. The big man could be seen complaining, as they went by, about being crammed into the little Subaru; they'd left his big Lexus behind. So they'll be coming back, without the Subaru. Over the water?

Becker's observation post was the parking lot of an Agway, a co-op farm and garden place, a hundred yards up the road from the turnoff to the Tooler cabins. He'd rented a red pickup truck two weeks ago, over in Kingston, the other side of the river, and during his observation hours he wore a yellow Caterpillar hat low over his eyes and sat lazily hunched in the passenger seat of the pickup, as though he was just the hired man and the boss was inside the Agway buying feed or tools or fencing or whatever. If he squinted a little, he could just barely see that dirt road turnoff down there.

So he could always see them come out. Sometimes they'd turn south, away from him, and then he'd scoot over behind the wheel, start the engine, and race after them. Other times, they'd head north, and he'd have leisure to eyeball them as they drove by, before setting off in pursuit.

But not today. No pursuit today. Today he knew where they were going, and what they planned to do, and where they planned to come afterward with the money. And Ray Becker would be there when they arrived.

Just in case, just to make absolutely sure none of them was coming back for any reason, he waited a full hour in the pickup in the Agway parking lot before at last he roused himself and slid over behind the wheel of the pickup and started the engine. Five after seven. The Agway closed on Fridays at seven, to catch the weekend gardeners and do-it-yourselfers, so the chain-link gate was half-shut; Becker steered around it, waved a happy goodbye to the kid in his Agway shirt and cap standing there waiting to shut the gate the rest of the way after the last customer finally drove on out, and the kid nodded back with employee dignity. Then Becker turned left and drove on down to the dirt road, and in.

This was the first he'd driven this road,

though he'd walked down it one night last week to spy on them, being damn careful not to make any noise, attract their attention. He'd found four cottages at the end of the road that night, but only one lit. He'd looked in windows long enough to get an idea of what their life was like in there, and he'd been surprised to see that the girl apparently slept alone. Two of the three men used the other two bedrooms, and the fake chauffeur bedded down on the sofa in the living room. There were guns visible in there, and maps, everything to confirm him in what he already knew: Howell had been right.

Now, just after seven in the evening on a Friday in late May, the sky still bright, late afternoon sunlight making long sharp black shadows that pointed at him through the woods, Ray Becker was back. As he drove along the dirt road toward the cabins, he visualized Marshall Howell as he'd been, the dying man in the wrecked Cadillac, and he grimaced yet again, feeling once more that quick twinge of embarrassment and shame.

He'd almost screwed it up but good that time. He'd known the man in the Cadillac was hurt and vulnerable, but he hadn't had any idea at all that he was in such bad shape, that he was dying.

Well, no, not dying, probably not dying. But killable, as it turned out, very easily killable.

Becker was in such a hurry at that instant.

He was the only lawman on the scene, but that couldn't last. Others had heard the same radio calls, would be coming to the same location, while the Feds continued in pursuit of the other vehicle. Ray Becker, understanding at once what it meant, had raced here at top speed when the radio call came in, because there was supposed to be a hundred forty thousand dollars in this car, and a hundred forty thousand dollars could save Ray Becker's ass. A hundred forty thousand dollars and his patrol car and he could be away and safe forever before they even noticed he was gone.

He'd already been thinking about it when the radio started squawking, thinking how the investigation was getting closer, how the detectives *knew* there must have been a local cop involved in that hijacking two months back, they just didn't know which one. But Ray Becker's reputation wasn't very good anyway, so they were focusing on him, and sooner or later they'd nail him, which was why he needed to get *away* from here, with a lot of money for a cushion. A hundred forty thousand dollars, say.

He almost broke his neck racing down that steep tumbled hillside through the freshly broken branches and crushed shrubs and scarred boulders to the crumpled wreck of the Cadillac, and when he got there the hundred forty thousand was gone. One perp left, crushed inside the car, bleeding and sweating

133

but conscious. Capable of speech.

'We don't have much time,' Becker told the son of a bitch, with his hand closing on the man's throat. 'Where's the money?'

'Don't—know.'

Lying, he had to be lying, he had to know where his partners were headed. Becker leaned on him, he did things to make the pain increase, and Howell moaned, and tears leaked from his eyes, but his story stayed the same. He didn't know where his partners were going, he didn't know where the money was.

'You got to give me something,' Becker told him, and all the rage he felt against the bastards that had double-crossed him and put him in this spot and cheated him out of his share of that other money, all of that rage made him bear down on this one, who finally broke and said, 'Some—thing—else.'

'What? Another robbery? More money?'

'Yes.'

'Quick.'

'All—knee. New. York. Cat . . .'

'What?'

'Cath—man. Wan—ted me.'

'For a heist. What heist? Quick!'

Howell's mouth opened again, but this time a great sack of blood came out, and burst down the front of the man, dark red and reeking, the heat of it making Becker recoil.

He hadn't known the man was that ~~close~~ to death. He hadn't intended to kill him, and

134

certainly not before he got all his answers, which made him feel stupid and inadequate and a failure then, and still did now. But then, as the man in the Cadillac's last breath came out full of blood, here came the Federals, leaping and sliding down the hill in their dark blue vinyl coats with the big yellow letters on the back, grabbing for holds one-handed, their machine pistols aimed upward at the sky.

Becker stepped back from the Cadillac. He called up to them, 'Take your time. They're gone. And so is this one.'

But Howell had come through after all, hadn't he? Becker had seen no choice but to follow through on Howell's lead, because he didn't have anything else, and it had all worked out. Hilliard Cathman. Then the one called Parker. Then the rest of them. Then the big white boat on the water, full of money, which *had* to be what they were here for.

It would be dark when they got back with the cash, so no need to hide the pickup. He left it between two of the cabins that weren't in use, then walked into the one they'd occupied. There was no locking these places, and they hadn't bothered to try, so Becker just opened the door and walked in.

Plenty of time. He walked through the place, saw they'd left nothing personal at all, saw they'd taken all the guns but left a few of the maps. He went into the kitchen and opened the refrigerator and there was beer in there, but he wouldn't be drinking anything until after. He'd need to be at his best tonight.

Gatorade, a big bottle of it, pale green. That was probably the big one. Kill him first. Kill the girl last.

Becker carried the Gatorade and a glass into the living room, turned on the television set, sat down. He looked at the picture when it came up, and abruptly laughed. The damn thing was black and white.

2

The reason Susan Cahill was so good at handling VIPs was that she understood the question of sex. With female VIPs you were— discreetly—hot tamales together under the skin, each acknowledging and admiring the allure of the other, becoming confidants and co-conspirators in the ongoing war of women to carve out a place for themselves in a male-dominated world, armed with nothing more than nerve and sex appeal. It worked; with the baggiest old crone, it still worked.

As for the male VIPs, they were even simpler. You turned on a little sex, a few smiles, a sidelong look or two, some body stretching. Enough to keep their minds focused, but not enough that anybody would lose their dignity. It was a nice tightrope to walk, and by now Susan could do it blindfolded.

She'd started, twelve years ago, as a flight attendant, where the most important skill you could learn, or be born with, was the non-aggressive manipulation of other human beings. She'd been very good at the job, keeping everybody happy at thirty-one thousand feet, and she'd also been very good-looking, and soon she was assigned to one of the choice transatlantic routes, Chicago–Milan. Her love affairs were with pilots or with amusing Italian businessmen. She made decent money, she had a nice high-rise apartment in the Loop overlooking Lake Michigan, she was having a good time, and then she made the one mistake. She'd seen others do it, and knew they were wrong, and knew it was stupid, and yet she did it herself. She fell in love with a passenger.

A banker, named Culver, based in Chicago. She fell in love with him, and took vacations with him, and said yes when he asked her to marry him, and quit the airline to spend more time with him, and then he said they'd be getting together forever just as soon as his divorce came through, which was the first she'd heard there already was a Mrs Culver. Of course there would never be a divorce, and of course he would be prepared to keep her set up in a much better apartment in the same building, and of course there was a hiring freeze at the airline when she asked for her old job back.

Well, we learn from our mistakes. Susan had had this current job, customer relations with Avenue Resorts, for three years now, and she firmly understood that her job was *not* to have relations with the customers, so she didn't. She knew that Avenue Resorts, even though its management was clean enough to pass any state gaming commission inspection, was mobbed up in some deep echelon of its command, but the fact of the mob didn't have anything to do with her work and didn't impinge on her in any way. The people of Avenue appreciated her, and she appreciated them, and that was that.

For three years she'd enjoyed her nice little house along the canal outside Biloxi, and she was sure she'd enjoy the nice house she'd just bought along the river south of Saratoga Springs, home of the famous racecourse, less than an hour commute from the boat. Mr Culver the banker had tried to clip the airline attendant's wings, but it hadn't worked. And it wasn't going to work, ever again.

Take Assemblyman Kotkind. At first, he'd tried to be grumpy, insisting on being met on the pier and escorted aboard, defiantly announcing the presence of his armed 'aides,' two state cops in civvies, all muscle and gun, no brain. She'd rolled with the initial punches, turned up the sex just a little bit, and in no time at all Assemblyman Kotkind was giving her sidelong looks of his own and having a little trouble concentrating on the job at hand.

Which was, she knew, what the politicians call repositioning. When a question is still undecided, a politician can have any opinion at all on the subject, but once the matter is settled, there's only one place for a politician to be: with the majority. Whatever Assemblyman Kotkind might personally think about legal gambling, he'd been publicly opposed to it, probably because that played well in his district, but now legal gambling was a fact, and the sky had not fallen, and it was time for Assemblyman Kotkind to be retroactively judicious.

On the other side, it was very much in Avenue's interests to butter up this assemblyman, to help him in his effort to switch horses in midstream without getting wet. As it says in the Bible, there's more joy when we get one to switch over to us than there is for the ninety-nine we've already got in our pocket. Therefore, 'I am yours to command,' Susan told the assemblyman, with her most professional smile.

'I just want to see for myself what the attraction is here,' the assemblyman said, looking at the front of her blouse. He was short enough to do that without being really obvious about it.

She took a deep breath, and turned slightly

into profile, also not really being obvious about it. 'That's what we're here for,' she assured him. 'You look us over as much as you want. Avenue Resorts wants you to see everything on this ship.'

'Good,' the assemblyman said, and blinked.

'And you'll find—this way, Mister Assemblyman—our first consideration is always safety.'

He gave her a different kind of look, considerably more jaundiced. 'Not money?'

She laughed lightly. 'That's our second consideration,' she said. 'Safety first, profit second. We'll take this elevator up to the sundeck, you'll get a better idea of what's happening.'

It was a fairly tight squeeze in the elevator, but everybody managed to keep some distance between bodies, even the assemblyman. Riding up, Susan explained the nomenclature of the three decks: sundeck on top, open to the air; boat deck below that, the enclosed promenade with the lifeboats suspended outside; main deck below that, with the restaurants on the outside and the casino within.

At this point, they had the sundeck to themselves. The views up here were terrific, both up and down the river and westward toward Albany, the old and new buildings pressed to the steep slope upward, making a kind of elaborate necklace around the big old stone pile of the statehouse.

'Home sweet home,' Susan suggested, with a gesture toward that massive stone building.

'I've seen it before,' the assemblyman told her, being gruff again. 'Tell me what's happening now.'

'Come to the rail.'

She and the assemblyman stood at the rail, with the two state cops on the assemblyman's other side. The ship was still tied up at the dock, and would remain there for another five or ten minutes. 'First we have our safety drill, then the cruise begins,' she explained. 'The *Spirit of the Hudson* has never sunk, and never will, but we want to be sure everybody's prepared just in case the unthinkable ever does happen. You see the lifeboats directly below us.'

The assemblyman agreed, he did see them there.

'You see the crew opening the glass doors along the promenade. Every passenger's ticket contains a code giving the location of the lifeboat that passenger should go to in case of emergency. The crew members down there are explaining lifeboat procedures now, and showing them the compartments on the inner wall containing life jackets. We don't ask the passengers to try on the jackets, but crew members down there do demonstrate how it's done.'

'If this unthinkable of yours does happen,' the assemblyman said, 'and this unsinkable tub

141

sinks, which is our lifeboat?'

Well, she could see she was going to have to do a whole lot of tinkling laughter with this little bastard before the day was done. 'Why, Assemblyman Kotkind,' she said, 'naturally you *and* I would be on the captain's launch.'

'Ah, naturally,' he said. 'And speaking of the captain—'

'He wants you to join him for dinner,' she said hastily, knowing that the last thing Captain Andersen wanted while setting sail was some bad-tempered politician underfoot. 'You and your aides, of course,' she added.

'Of course,' the assemblyman said, while the 'aides' continued to stand around looking blankfaced and correct. Poor guys, she thought, giving them some of her attention for the first time. If six hours with this gnome is going to be tough for me, what must it be like for them?

3

Dan Wycza thought this woman Susan Cahill would be therapeutic. She looked like somebody who liked sex without getting all bent out of shape over it, somebody who knew what it was for and all about its limitations. Look how she was giving Lou Sternberg those flashing eyes and teeth, those tiny bumps and

142

grinds, not as a come-on but as a method of control, like the bullfighter's red cape. Wycza knew Sternberg would be enjoying the show and at the same time he'd enjoy pretending to be taken in by the show. The bluffer bluffed.

Meanwhile, from the sidelines, Wycza could watch Susan Cahill strut her stuff and think to himself that she would certainly be therapeutic. A good healthy roll in the hay.

Health was extremely important to Dan Wycza. It was, as the man said, all we've got. His body was important to him the way Mike Carlow considered those race cars of his important. Take care of it, keep it finely tuned, and it will do the job for you. The way a car nut likes to tinker with the engine, the fuel mixture, the tire pressure, all those details, that's the way Dan Wycza took care of himself. His diet was specific and controlled, his exercise lengthy and carefully planned. He traveled with so many pills, so many minerals and herbs and dietary supplements, that he seemed like either a hypochondriac or the healthiest-looking invalid in history, but it was all just to keep the machine well tuned.

And sex was a part of it. Simple uncomplicated sex was good for both the body and the mind. There was nothing like rolling around with a good willing woman to keep the blood flowing and the mental attitude perked up. A woman like this Susan Cahill, for instance.

143

Pity it wasn't going to happen. This woman would never fuck anything but power, or at least her idea of power. At the moment, to her, Dan Wycza, aka Trooper Helsing, was just a spear carrier, part of the furniture, a nothing. Later, he'd be something, all right, but it wasn't likely to be something she'd find a turn-on. Not likely.

For the moment, he and Parker were just doing their dumb-fuck thing, trailing along behind Lou Sternberg while the Cahill woman showed him a little of this and a little of that. Wycza remembered this ship from when he'd been a sucker aboard her, that one time, down in Biloxi. (The healthy woman he was with at the time liked to gamble.) It looked exactly the same, the carpets, the colors of the walls, the shapes of the doors, the edgings around the windows. The only difference was the uniform on the various crew members who worked in public; the pursers, dealers, hostesses, managers. When the ship was the *Spirit of Biloxi*, the uniforms were tan with dark red; sort of the colors of Mississippi dirt. Now that she was the *Spirit of the Hudson*, operating in the Empire State, the uniforms were royal blue with gold. But some of the people inside those uniforms were the same, he was sure of it.

Once the joke of a safety drill was done down on the boat deck, and the ship at last eased away from the dock to start its leisurely amble downstream, Cahill became a little less flirty and more matter-of-fact. 'Of course I *will* be taking you around for a complete tour of the ship,' she said, 'but first I know Captain Andersen wants to greet you. He wasn't able to before this, of course. Departure and arrival are his really busy times.'

'I'll be happy to meet him,' Sternberg told her, and as she set off across the boat deck toward the bridge, the others following her, he asked, 'Was he the captain before? When it was down South?'

'Oh, yes,' she said, sounding delighted by the fact that it was the same captain. 'Captain Andersen's been with the company for seven years. Longer than I have!' And she did that girlish laugh thing of hers again.

The bridge was amidships, up one steep metal stairway from the sun deck. Everything up here was metal, thickly painted white. The bridge itself was two long narrow rooms, the one in front featuring an oval wall of glass to give a full hundred-eighty-degree view of everything ahead of the ship and to both sides. The helm was here, and the computers and communications links that made the function of captain almost unnecessary these days. Tell the machine where you want to go, and get out of its way.

The rear room, also full of windows but without the oval, was a kind of office and rest area; two gray vinyl sofas sat among the desks and maps and computer screens. This is where the stairway led, and this is where Captain Andersen stood, splendid in his navy blue uniform with the gold stripes and his white officer's hat with the black brim, as though he were about to lead this ship on a perilous journey around the world, pole to pole, instead of merely a pokey stroll to nowhere; Albany, New York, to Albany, New York, in six hours.

His back was to the open doorway, and he was conferring with three others, two dressed AS officers, one as crew. He turned at their entrance, and he was a Scandinavian, or he wanted you to think he was. Tall and pale-haired, he had pale eyebrows and pale blue eyes and a large narrow pale nose. He wore the least possible beard; a narrow amber line down and forward from both ears to define his jaw, and no mustache. In his left hand he held a gnarled old dark-wood pipe.

Cahill did the honors: 'Captain Lief Andersen, I'd like to introduce Assemblyman Morton Kotkind of the New York State legislature.'

They both said how-do-you-do, and shook hands, Sternberg with grumpy dignity, Andersen with a more aloof style. 'You have a beautiful ship, captain,' Sternberg told him, as though forced to admit it.

'And you have a beautiful statehouse,' the captain assured him, nodding his narrow beak at it.

146

They all turned to look, even Wycza, who usually ignored polite crap like that, and it was still there all right, slowly receding. It was now quarter past eight, and though the sun hadn't yet set it was behind the Albany hills, putting the eastern slopes of the city in shade, so that the statehouse looked more than ever like simply a huge pile of rocks.

Sternberg said, 'It's all right, I suppose. It's always been a little too much like a castle for me. I'm too instinctive a small "d" democrat for that.'

'The schloss, yes,' the captain agreed. 'I quite understand. That may be why I like it. There was nothing in Biloxi like that.'

'No, there wouldn't be.'

'I understand,' the captain said, 'your associates here carry weapons. As you know, on the ship—'

'That was all taken care of,' Sternberg broke in, and Wycza thought, now what.

'I'm sorry, Mister Assemblyman,' the captain said, with the faint smile of someone whose decisions are never argued with, 'but the company has strict—'

'This was dealt with,' Sternberg insisted, showing a little more impatience, almost a touch of anger, 'when the arrangements were made.'

'If you were told—' the captain began, but then Parker, standing next to Wycza here in the background, interrupted him, saying,

147

'Captain, Trooper Helsing and I apologize, but we have no choice. We are not permitted to be disarmed while on duty. It's regulations. You could phone our barracks in Albany, speak to the major—'

Holy shit, Parker, Wycza thought, what if he does? What if he even asks for the phone number? Jesus, this was supposed to be solved, the fucking guns are the reason we're playing this dumb game. What are we supposed to do now, shoot our way off the ship? Or hand over the goddam guns and play-act the whole evening and never get to do the caper. Walk into the money room and out again, say thank you very much, and go off somewhere and shoot ourselves in the head.

But before Parker could finish his offer, and before they could know whether or not the captain would have taken him up on it, Sternberg burst in, furious, and now furious at Parker: 'Renfield, what's the matter with you? One phone call to the barracks about me being on this ship, and *why*, and *all* of our security is destroyed. The *press* is there, Renfield! The press is always in those offices.'

'Oh.' Wycza had never seen Parker look abashed, and wouldn't have guessed he knew how to do it, but he did. 'Sorry, Mr Kotkind,' he said, with that abashed face. 'I didn't think.'

Sternberg turned a glowering eye on Susan Cahill: 'Ms Cahill, my office made these arrangements with—'

'Yes, yes, you did,' she said, and Wycza felt almost sorry for her. She was between a rock and a hard place, and she hadn't known this was going to happen. She said, 'Just give me a minute, Mister Assemblyman,' and turned away, to say, quiet but intense, 'Captain Andersen, could we talk for just a minute?'

'Susan,' the captain said, 'you *know*—'

'Yes, yes, but if we could just—'

'There's a perfectly adequate safe in that corner right there, no risk could—'

'Captain.'

And finally, not merely holding his arm but stroking the upper arm from elbow to shoulder, up and down, up and down, she managed to turn the captain away as though he were the ship itself and she the small but powerful tugboat, and she walked him away into the forward room, the one with the oval wall of windows.

Once they were out of sight, Sternberg turned on Parker and hissed, 'You *know* there's to be no publicity about this! You *understood* that!'

Playing it out, Wycza knew, for the benefit of the other crew members in the room, all of whom were pretending to be busy at other things but were clearly listening with all their ears. Still, as Wycza guessed, Parker could play at this game only so far. He'd gone back to his usual stone face, and all he said was, 'Yes, sir. I think Ms Cahill will straighten it out.' Enough is enough, in other words.

Sternberg understood the message, and contented himself with a few harrumphs and a couple of glowers in the general direction of the receding city, until a much more cheerful Susan Cahill came back into the room, trailed by a discontented Captain Andersen holding fast to his dignity. 'All settled,' she announced. 'But you see now, Mister Assemblyman, just how careful we are on this ship.' Immediately spinning the scene from confrontation to a positive message.

'And I'm glad you are,' Sternberg told her, gallantly accepting the spin. 'I'm sorry, Captain,' he said, 'if the special circumstances of this tour mean we have to bend a rule or two. I think you'll agree it's in a good cause'

The captain unbent himself, not without difficulty. 'I'm sure it is a good cause, Assemblyman Kotkind,' he said, with a small bow. 'We are newly arrived in your part of the world, we hope to become good neighbors and to be accepted by all our new friends, as time goes on. For that to be true, I realize, we will have to learn something of your ways. But for now, do follow Susan, let her show you this quite lovely ship, and although you are here for serious business, please do take pleasure in the scenery as we pass by.'

'I will,' Sternberg promised. 'Delighted to meet you, Captain.'

'And you, Mister Assemblyman. I

understand we'll be dining together. I look forward to it.'

'As do I. We won't keep you, Captain, I know you're busy.'

As they were leaving, the captain even found a smile to show Parker and Wycza. 'I certainly hope, gentlemen,' he said, 'we shall not be *seeing* those weapons of yours.'

Wycza grinned at him. He knew how to handle a soft lob like that. 'If you see my weapon on this ship, Captain,' he said, 'I'm not doing my job.'

4

Ray Becker sat in an old wooden Adirondack chair on the screened porch at the back of the cabin, the bottle of Gatorade at his side, and watched the sunset over the river. It's a new day, he thought. I'm starting over, and this time I'm gonna get it right.

He was a fuckup, and he knew it. He'd been a fuckup all his life, third of five sons of a hardware store owner who was never any problem for any of his boys so long as they worked their ass off. Being in the middle, Ray had never been big enough or strong enough to compete with his meaner older brothers, and never been cute enough or sly enough to compete with his guileful younger brothers, so he was just the fuckup in the middle, and grew up knowing that about himself, and had never done anything in his life to make him change his opinion of himself.

God knows he tried. He liked the Army, for instance. Go in there and do your job and don't sweat about promotion, and the Army was never any problem for anybody, so long as they worked their ass off. But drink and bad companions have taken down many a better man than Ray Becker, and he did wind up with a bunch of clowns that had it in mind to rob the base PX, and of course they got caught, and of course Ray was the first to crack, so of course he was the one who wound up with the deal and testified against everybody else, and they went to Leavenworth while he didn't even have a bad mark on his record; a general discharge under honorable conditions. Only the Army wouldn't ever want him back.

Policing turned out to be like the Army, only with different-colored uniforms. But the concept was the same; a strict set of rules, easy to understand. Stay within them, you'll be all right. And in police work, particularly small-town police work, you didn't even have to work your ass off.

But the other little glitch was money. The old man had been as cheap a son of a bitch as it was possible to find, and still was, no doubt; Ray had had no contact at all with the family for more than ten years. What would be in it for him? Work for the old man, and get nothing out of it. The only reason the old man would know Ray wasn't there was if he had to get somebody else to do the heavy lifting.

Thirty-seven years old. A born fuckup who didn't really want much in life, but who simply couldn't keep himself from conniving. Show him a rule, and he'll say, 'Oh, thank God, there's rules,' and absolutely mean it, and at the same time scheme from the get-go for some sneaky way to get around the rule, subvert it, defy it and ignore it. Maybe that was an inheritance from the old man, too.

Well, Ray Becker's fuckup days were done. This last one was the lesson, for good and all. Four million dollars in commercial paper being trucked north to Chicago out of some bank that went bust down south. A big tractor-trailer full of valuable paper and a handful of armed guards. Two unmarked cars, one ahead and one behind, with more armed guards, and here it all came, stitching up the center of the country, heading for the big stone banks of Chicago, America's Switzerland.

Who knew about this movement of so much valuable paper? Hundreds of people, all of them supposed to be trustworthy. Bank people, the security service that provided the guards, various federal agencies, and police forces along the way, that had to be told what was happening in their territory, as a courtesy and for practical reasons, too.

Ray had no idea who set up the job, but one of the gang was an old pal of his from Army days, one of the boys he'd sent to Leavenworth, who was out now and had joined up with a much more serious bunch of heist artists. Old pal Phil had found his way to Ray Becker to tell him he was prepared to forgive and forget the old Army days because old pal Ray was going to feed old pal Phil the information on how the truck full of valuable paper was coming through; what time of what day on what road with what additional escort. And just to show there were no hard feelings, Ray's share was going to be two hundred thousand dollars. A nice little nest egg. And just to show this was all in earnest, old pal Phil was handing old pal Ray a thousand dollars, ten new one-hundred-dollar bills, on account.

On account of that was all he was going to get.

The final fuckup. Make a four-million-dollar robbery possible, get one measly miserable thousand dollars out of it, and be the only one who gets caught and goes to jail for it.

Not this time. This time luck had been with him, for once. This time, he thought he'd been given the hundred forty thousand dollars that would help him clear out and start over under another identity somewhere else, but instead he'd been given Marshall Howell, and then Hilliard Cathman, and then Parker and the others, and then the gambling boat.

Spirit of the Hudson. Luck is with me at long last, Ray Becker thought. So maybe I'll take a little of tonight's money, some time soon, take a ride on that gambling boat, see what happens. Not all of it, for God's sake, not even a lot of it, not to fuck up all over again. Take a couple thousand, that's all, see if my luck holds. Win some money, meet some nice blonde woman in a long dress with her tits hanging out at the top, drink a glass of champagne. Buy a necktie before I go.

Across the way, the sun had ratcheted down out of sight. The sky over there was deep red above the jagged black masses of the Catskills, with blackness below, pierced by a few pinholes of yellow light. And here came the boat, the very boat itself, gliding down the river, just *exuding* light. Spreading a pale halo out over the water and the air, a misty milky glow that made it look like a ship from some other universe, a mirage, floating into our plain dark world. Faintly, he could hear music, he could see people move around on the ship, the beautiful white boat surrounded by its veil of light.

And you're coming for *me*, he thought, whether you know it or not. He smiled at the ship. In his mind, the blonde woman leaned toward him, and she smiled, too.

5

For Greg Manchester, it was almost like being a spy. Here he was, on the *Spirit of the Hudson*, anonymous with his tiny pocket Minolta camera and his even smaller palm-of-the-hand audio cassette recorder, snapping pictures here and there around the ship, murmuring observations and data into the recorder, and nobody at all had the first idea he was a reporter.

And the funny thing was, he didn't even intend a negative story. It was just that the management of this ship, Avenue Resorts, based in Houston, Texas, was so antsy about the controversial nature of casino gambling that they demanded total control over every facet of any news story involving them, or they would withhold all cooperation.

It was easy for the management to enforce that policy with television newspeople, of course, because television newspeople necessarily travel with so much gear, cameras and recording equipment and lights and all the rest of it, that they need cooperation everywhere they go. But Greg Manchester worked in the world of print, a reporter with the Poughkeepsie *Journal*, a daily paper in the town that just happened to be the *Spirit of the Hudson's* southern terminus, and Greg

Manchester was determined to get a story that was not made dull and bland and predictable by an excess of cooperation with Avenue Resorts.

His editor had been skeptical at first, since the *Spirit of the Hudson* was already an important advertiser, but Greg had said, 'Jim, I'm not doing an exposé. What's to expose? They're a clean operation. This will just be fun for the readers, to be a fly on the wall for one cruise of the glamorous ship.'

'No controversy,' Jim said.

'No controversy,' Greg promised.

Well, it was an easy promise to keep. With the *Spirit of the Hudson*, with so much official oversight and political grandstanding all around it, everything was absolutely squeaky clean, from the place settings to the morals of the crew. So what Greg was doing was essentially human interest, which quite naturally led him to the girl in the wheelchair.

Poor goddam thing, he wanted to hug her or something. She looked to be in her late twenties, the same as him, but so frail, so vulnerable, and yet so brave. If he wasn't careful, she'd take over the place, and he didn't want that. She'd be in it, of course, a part of it, but the story still had to be about the ship.

So he limited himself in the early hours of the cruise to one brief conversation with the girl in the wheelchair and the rather tough-looking man in a chauffeur's uniform who wheeled her around. They were out on the promenade deck at that time, watching the shoreline go by, and he went over just to make a little small talk—lucky in the weather, beautiful scenery, that kind of thing, just to establish a connection—and they were both gracious, but she was obviously very weak and not up to too much talk, so soon he moved on, looked at other things, took pictures here and there (a few of the wheelchair girl, too, of course, and he'd have to learn her name before the cruise was over), and made his observations into the recorder.

There was somebody else of interest aboard, too, a VIP of some sort, an ill-tempered kind of guy with a couple of bruisers who looked like they must be bodyguards, all being escorted around by Susan Cahill. He remembered Susan Cahill, though she'd have no reason to remember him, from the press conferences when the ship first arrived, when he'd just been a part of the herd of reporters all being schmoozed at once. Susan Cahill was sexy and smart and tough as nails, and Greg could see she was treating this short fat sour-looking man with the softest of kid gloves. Somebody important, at least to the *Spirit of the Hudson.*

He took pictures in the better dining room, on the port side of the ship, but actually ate in the sandwich joint on the other side, since he didn't have an expense account for this little jaunt. He visited the casino but didn't play, and noticed that the craps tables were the most popular (and the loudest) and the two roulette wheels the least. Six blackjack tables were open, three with a ten-dollar minimum and three with a twenty-five dollar minimum, and all did well. The rows of slot machines were almost all occupied almost all of the time, but the video poker games didn't draw as big a crowd.

The ship arrived at Poughkeepsie a little before eleven, and would stay at the dock for ten minutes. Now Greg was sorry he hadn't taken the train up to Albany; if he had, he could get off now, because he had just about everything he needed for his story, except the name of the girl in the wheelchair and the identity of the VIP, which would take no time at all. But he'd driven up this afternoon, so his car was up there, so he had to do the round-trip. But that was okay, there could still be more to learn.

A little after eleven, the ship steamed out away from Poughkeepsie, made a long curving arc out to the middle of the river, then slowly pivoted on its axis there, while the customers who could tear themselves away from the gaming tables crowded along the rails to stare, until the prow was finally pointed upstream, white foam now giving it an Edwardian collar as the ship's engines deepened their hum and they started up against the current.

Well, he might as well get his two 'who' questions answered, so as the lights of Poughkeepsie faded in the night darkness behind them Greg went looking for the girl in the wheelchair and his VIP.

He found the VIP first, in the casino, with his bodyguards and Susan Cahill, glowering in disapproval at the roulette wheels. The floor manager, a neat young guy in the royal blue and gold uniform of the ship, stood at parade rest just inside the casino door, and Greg approached him, saying, 'Excuse me. That must be somebody important, I guess.'

'*He* thinks so,' the floor manager said. He had some sort of southern accent.

Greg laughed. 'Who does he think he is?'

'New York State assemblyman,' the floor manager said. 'Not that big a deal, I wouldn't think. Name's Kotkind, he's from Brooklyn.'

Greg blinked, and stared at the VIP and his entourage across the way. 'Are you sure?'

'Absolutely,' the floor manager said, and took a business card out of his shirt pocket. 'Gave me his card, you see? Handing them out to anybody in the crew he talks to. I told him I don't vote in his district, and he said that's okay, when he runs for statewide office I can vote for him then. Pretty pleased with himself, huh?'

Greg looked at the card, and it was Assemblyman Morton Kotkind's card, sure enough; he'd seen it before. 'Well, I'll be damned,' he said. 'Thanks.' And he left there, to try to think this out. What the heck was going on here?

Coming out of the casino, he was just in time to see the nearby elevator door close, with the girl in the wheelchair and her chauffeur companion inside. Going up. He's the one I'll talk to, Greg thought. He felt confused, and didn't want to blow his cover or make a stupid mistake, so he felt he needed somebody to discuss the thing with, and that chauffeur had struck him right away as a competent no-nonsense kind of guy.

Up the stairs he went, and saw the chauffeur just pushing the wheelchair out on to the glass-enclosed promenade. Greg followed, and found very few people up here now, there being so little to see at night, except the few lights of little river towns. The chauffeur pushed the wheelchair slowly along, in no hurry, apparently just to keep in motion. Greg hurried to catch up.

6

Mike Carlow was glad this was the last night. He'd been pushing this damn wheelchair around for over a week, carrying Noelle's slops into the men's room, doing his strong silent (but caring) number, and he was bored with it.

Also, just pushing the wheelchair got to be a drag. But he'd learned early the first night out that he had to keep the wheelchair moving. Stop somewhere, and the sympathetic people started hovering around, asking questions, being pains in the ass. Noelle could pitch a faint every once in a while to make them lay off, but that was work, too. It was simpler to just keep moving.

Of course, even then you still got the pushy ones, of all types, old and young, male and female. Of them, Carlow thought he probably disliked the young males the worst, the ones who came on all sympathetic and concerned but you could see in their eyes that what they really wanted was to fuck Noelle's brains out.

Not that Carlow wanted Noelle for himself. He was meeting her for the first time on this job, he liked her, he thought she was stand-up and could be counted on, but she wasn't the kind of woman who appealed to him in that other way. For that, he liked a heftier woman, someone out of his own world, the kind you'd meet in the auto race circuit, who could change a tire and whose favorite food was pancakes.

For Mike Carlow, everything related back to the track and the fast cars. He'd driven his first race when he was fourteen, won for the first time when he was sixteen, and had never much cared about anything else. For

162

instance, he'd figured it out early that the amount of gasoline in the gas tank affected the car's center of gravity, constantly shifting the center of gravity as the fuel was used up, so while still in high school he'd designed a car that wouldn't have that problem because there wasn't any gas tank; the car was built around a frame of hollow aluminium tubing, and the tubing held the gas. When someone told him it was crazy to want to drive a car where he'd be completely surrounded by gasoline, he'd said, 'So what?' He still couldn't see what was wrong with the idea, and didn't understand why no official at any track in America would permit such a design into a race.

Still, there were other cars and other designs, that they *would* accept, so Carlow was reasonably happy. Every year or so he took a job like this one, to raise the money to build more race cars, and every year, one way or another, he survived both his obsession with race cars and the heists he went on to support that obsession.

'Excuse me.'

Carlow looked around and it was one of the young studs, in fact one that had hit on them earlier in the evening until Noelle had gone all faint on him. Not wanting to have to deal with the same guy twice in one outing, and also feeling some of the impatience that comes when you know the job is almost finished, and feeling ill-used because he'd come up here to the promenade because it wasn't full of annoying people after dark, Carlow gave him a pretty icy look and said, 'Yes?'

'Do you mind?' The guy was young and eager like before, but now he also seemed troubled. 'I need to talk to somebody,' he said, 'and I was going to come see you two, anyway. I'm just not sure what to do.'

The promenade had benches along the inner wall, but the rest was clear. Down ahead toward the stern, a few people strolled along, moving away. Back toward the prow, an exhausted older couple sat on a bench barely awake. Carlow took all this in because he had a sense for this kind of problem when he was on a job, a sense that told him when there was a rip in the fabric, and he just had the feeling there was a rip in the fabric coming right now. The question was, what had gone wrong, and what could they do about it? 'Sure,' he said. 'Why don't you sit on the bench here so Jane Ann can be part of the conversation?'

'All right.'

The guy sat, looking disturbed, confused about something, and Carlow arranged the wheelchair and himself so the guy was hard to see from either direction along the promenade. 'Tell us about it,' he suggested.

'Well, the thing is,' the guy said, 'I'm here sort of secretly, and I'm not sure if I should blow my cover.'

Carlow said, 'You mean, you're not an

164

ordinary passenger, you're not what you seem to be, you're something else.' A cop? Not a chance.

'That's right, My name's Greg Manchester, and I'm a reporter, and I'm doing a—'

Noelle snapped, with more sharpness than her frail condition would allow, 'A reporter?'

Manchester was too involved in his own problems to notice Noelle's slip. He said, 'The cruise line company won't permit unescorted reporters, so I just want to do a fly on the wall kind of thing. Not negative, just fun.'

Carlow said, 'So you're going around looking at things, making notes . . .'

'And taking pictures, too,' Manchester said. 'When nobody's looking.' To Noelle he said, 'That's why I was coming to you anyway, to get your name.'

Noelle said, 'You have pictures of *me*? Oh, I wouldn't like that, the way I look—'

'You're *beautiful*, Miss— Jane Ann, is it?'

Carlow said, 'But then something else happened. What?'

'There's a VIP on the ship, I don't know if you—'

'Yeah, we've seen him,' Carlow said, thinking, this is it. This is it right here. 'What about him?'

'Well, he says he's a state assemblyman named Kotkind,' Manchester said, 'but he isn't. He's a fake. I know Assemblyman Kotkind, I've interviewed him.'

165

'Ah,' Carlow said.

'What I can't figure out,' Manchester said, 'is why anybody would *do* that. Did the real assemblyman send this guy in his place? He is handing out the assemblyman's business card. If I say something, *my* cover is blown and maybe I just make a fool of myself. Or maybe something's wrong, and the cruise line should know about it. What do you think?'

Noelle said, 'I think—' and began to cough. She tried to go on talking through the coughs that wracked her poor frail body, and Manchester leaned closer to her, concerned, trying to make out what she was trying to say.

Carlow kept his wallet in his inside jacket pocket because he kept his sap in his right hip pocket; a black leather bag full of sand. It was one smooth movement to reach back, draw it out, lift it up, drop it down, and put Mr Manchester on ice.

Noelle's left arm shot out, her hand splayed against Manchester's chest, and she held him upright on the bench. 'Don't kill him,' she said.

'Of course not,' Carlow told her. He knew as well as she did that the law goes after a killer a lot more determinedly than it goes after a heister. If it were possible to keep this clown alive, Carlow would do it. He said, 'I need a gag, and I need something to tie him.'

'You hold him for a minute.'

Carlow pushed the wheelchair a few inches forward, and sat on the bench beside the

166

clown. He put his left elbow up on to the guy's chest and said, 'Okay.'

Noelle was wearing all these filmy garments out of a gothic novel, so now she reached down inside and gritted her teeth and Carlow heard a series of rips. Out she came with several lengths of white cloth, and handed them to him. 'I've got him now,' she said, and put her hand on Manchester's chest again.

Carlow bent to tie the ankles together, then tied the wrists behind the back, then stuffed a ball of cloth into Manchester's mouth and used the last strip to make a gag.

Noelle said, 'What are you going to do with him?'

'Lifeboat.'

They'd watched that damn safety drill every night for over a week, so Carlow knew exactly how to open the sliding glass door and how to open one segment of the top of the enclosed lifeboat just below. 'You keep him,' he said, and started to rise.

'Wait!'

'For what?'

'Damn it, Mike,' she said. 'Get the camera. That's *my* face he's got there, and probably yours, too.'

'Oh. Sorry.'

Carlow sat again, and patted him down, and found first the cassette recorder and then the Minolta. 'Nice camera,' he commented, and pocketed both.

He looked around. The half-asleep couple were still in the same spot. Toward the stern, three or four people were looking out and downriver at where they'd been, talking together. Carlow stood, crossed to the outer glass wall, slid open a panel, stepped through on to the curved roof of the lifeboat, leaned down, gave the stiff handle a quarter turn, lifted, and a rectangular piece of the roof opened right up. Then he crossed back to Noelle, sat beside Manchester again, and said, 'Now I have to get him over there.'

'Put him on my lap,' she said, 'and wheel us over.'

'Nice.'

He held Manchester while Noelle wheeled herself backward out of the way. Then he stood, picked up Manchester under the armpits and placed him seated on top of Noelle. 'So this is what they call a dead weight,' Noelle said.

Carlow wheeled them both across the promenade to the open glass door, where the cool night air now drifted in. He stopped, and she shoved, and Manchester went toppling out and down into the lifeboat. Carlow winced. He'd land on a stack of life preservers, but still. 'Goodbye,' Noelle said.

'He'll have a headache in the morning,' Carlow commented, as he moved the wheelchair to one side so he could shut everything up again.

'Let him take a picture of *that*,' she said, unsympathetic. 'Asshole.'

7

Susan Cahill didn't really like Morton Kotkind, Lou Sternberg could tell. She smiled at him, she waved her tits at him, she smoothed the way for him as they made their long slow inspection tour of the ship, she even went out of her way to chat with him during dinner at the captain's table, since the captain himself was making every effort *not* to be friendly and accommodating but was instead doing a very good impression of an iceberg from his native land; and yet, Sternberg could tell, Susan Cahill didn't really like Morton Kotkind.

Which was fine with Sternberg, who hadn't liked Kotkind either, during those days in the lawyers' bar on Court Street in Brooklyn, getting to know the man, getting to know him so well it was an absolute pleasure to feed him the Mickey Finn yesterday. Probably, Sternberg thought, Cahill would be just as happy to feed a Mickey to *me*, and the thought made him smile.

Cahill picked up on that, and smiled right back, across the dinner table. 'Mister Assemblyman,' she said, 'I believe you're enjoying yourself.'

169

'I'm not here to enjoy myself,' he snapped at her, and put his pouty brat face on again, which she bravely pretended not to see.

But in fact he was enjoying himself hugely, which was rare on a heist. For him, pleasure was at home, his little town house in London —2 Montpelier Gardens, SW6—with its little garden in the back enclosed by ancient stone walls, with roses to left and right, cucumbers and brussels sprouts at the back. There he lived, and in that city his friends lived, people who had nothing to do with any kind of criminality, except possibly in the tax forms they filled out for Inland Revenue.

That was an extra bonus in Sternberg's living arrangements; he filled out no tax forms anywhere. To be resident in the UK for more than six months, legally, one had to sign a statement that one will be supported from outside the country, will neither go on the dole nor take a job away from some native born Englishman. *How* the foreigner supports himself from outside the country doesn't matter, only that he does. So there was never a reason to deal with Inland Revenue. At the same time, since he didn't live or work in the US, didn't even pay any bills or credit accounts or mortgages there, he also flew below the IRS's radar. Which meant there was no one anywhere to say, 'Just how *do* you support yourself, Mr Sternberg?' Lovely.

In fact, it was the occasional job with a

trusted associate like Parker that took care of his material wants, while the house in Montpelier Gardens saw to his spiritual needs, so except for the occasional soulless transatlantic airplane ride he was a reasonably happy man, though you could never tell that from his face.

The airplane rides were necessitated by his iron rule that he would never work and live in the same territory. London—in fact, all of England—was out of bounds. Whenever it was time to restock the bank accounts, it was off to America once more, with Lillian the char left behind to see to the roses and the cucumbers; the brussels sprouts took care of themselves.

This particular journey to the land of his birth looked to be a fairly easy one, and profitable. The last time he'd worked with Parker it had been anything but profitable, but that hadn't been Parker's fault, and Sternberg didn't hold it against him. This job looked much more likely to provide another year or two of comfort in SW6.

The problem with the job was that it was taking too long. Sternberg had pretended to be other people before in the course of a heist—a telephone repairman, a fire department inspector—but never for five hours. From eight P.M. fill one A.M., in this confined space on the *Spirit of the Hudson*, essentially on his own since Parker and Wycza's job was just to stand around looking tough and competent;

Lou Sternberg not only had to be a politician and a Brooklynite, he also had to be a bad-tempered boor. He actually was bad-tempered at times, he had to admit, but he'd never been a politician or a Brooklynite, and he certainly hoped he had never been a boor.

Ah, well. Dinner passed, the turnaround at Poughkeepsie passed, the inspections of the casino and the kitchens and the purser's office and the promenades and the game room and the laughable library and all the rest of it slowly passed. The engine room was interesting, being more like a windowless control tower than like anything purporting to be a steamship's engine room Sternberg had ever seen in the movies. And through it all, he maintained this sour and offensive persona.

There were reasons for it. First, the original was like this. Second, bad temper keeps other people off balance, and they never believe the person being difficult is *lying* in some way; rudeness is always seen as bona fide. And the third reason was the money room.

There'd been only one real fight so far, the one over the handguns, and Sternberg had won that, as he'd expected to. The money room would be another fight—*access* to the money room was almost certain to be a fight—and by the time they got there Sternberg wanted the entire ship's complement to be convinced that if they argued with this son of a bitch assemblyman, they lost.

Of course, if Susan Cahill had led them straight to the money room at nine-thirty or ten, it would have been a real waste, because most of the money wouldn't have arrived yet, but they'd assumed that she wouldn't want to mention the money room at all, and so far she hadn't.

Twelve-fifteen, and not a single goddam thing left to look at. The last place they inspected was the nurse's office, and found she was well equipped in there for first-level treatment of medical emergencies, and also had a direct-line radio to the medevac helicopter at Albany Hospital, probably for when winners had heart attacks. Sternberg stretched the moment by congratulating her on her readiness and enquiring into her previous work history, and unbent so far he could feel the curmudgeon façade start to crack.

So finally they came out of her office, and it was only twelve-fifteen, and Cahill said, 'Well, Mister Assemblyman, that's it. You've seen it all. And now, if you wouldn't consider it a bribe'—and she beamed on him, jolly and sexy—'the captain would love to buy you a drink.'

Sure he would. Too early, too early. What should he do? This was Sternberg's call alone, he couldn't confer with the other two, couldn't even take time to look at them. Accept a drink? Should he stall another half an hour that way, then all at once remember the money room and demand to see it? Or go with it now, knowing they'd be cutting their take by about forty-five minutes worth of money?

Go now, he decided. Go now because they were in a movement here, a flow, and it would be best to just keep it going, not let it break off and then later try to start it up again. And go now because he was tired of being Mister Assemblyman. 'We're not quite finished,' he said. 'When we *are* finished, if there's still time, I'll be very happy to join you and the captain— you will join us, won't you?—in a drink.'

Either she was bewildered, or she did bewilderment well. 'Not finished? But you've seen everything.'

'I haven't seen,' he said, 'where the money goes. It's still on the ship, is it not?'

She looked stricken. 'Oh, Mister Assemblyman, we can't do that.'

He gave her his most suspicious glare. 'Can't do what?'

'That room,' she said, 'you see, that room is completely closed away, for security reasons; *nobody* can get into that room.'

'Nonsense,' he said. 'There must be people in there. How do they get out?'

'They have their own door on the side of the ship,' she explained, 'with access direct to the dock and the armored car, when we land.'

He said, 'You're telling me there's no way in or out of that place, whatever the place is—'

'The money room,' she said. 'It's called the

money room.'

'Because that's the whole point of the operation, isn't it?' he demanded. 'The money. And *what happens to it next.*'

'Mister Assemblyman, the company's books are—'

'Very attractive, I have no doubt,' he interrupted. 'Ms Cahill, do you suddenly have something to hide from me? The very *crux* of this matter is what happens to gambling money once it has been lost to the casino operator.'

'Mister Kotkind,' she said, voice rising, forgetting to call him by his title, 'we hide *nothing* on this ship! Every penny is accounted for.'

'And yet you tell me there's no access to the, what did you call it, money room. And if this ship were to sink, the people in that money room would simply die? If it caught fire? Is *that* what you're telling me? You have human beings in that room, and their safety is at risk for *money?*'

'Of course not.' She was scrambling now, not sure how to stay ahead of him. 'They can unlock themselves out if it's absolutely necessary.'

'And unlock others in,' he insisted. 'I haven't even seen the *door* to this place. Is there—'

'It has its own staircase,' she said reluctantly, 'down from the restroom area, with a guard at the top and a *very* locked door at the bottom.'

'Oh, does it? And I assume that door has, like any apartment in my district in Brooklyn, an intercom beside the door, and a bell. You can ring that bell and explain the situation and they can open up and let me in to inspect that room and I can see for *myself* what's happening with that money.'

'Mister Ambas—Assemblyman, I . . .' She shook her head, and moved her hands around.

'And *without*,' he told her, as heavily as any prosecutor, 'warning them ahead of time that they are going to be observed.'

She'd run out of things to say, but she still didn't want to give in. She was desperate, confused, blindsided but not yet defeated. She stood staring at Sternberg, trying to find a way out.

No; no way out. He let the full flood of his exasperation wash over her: 'Ms Cahill, do I have to go to the *captain*? This absolutely *core* part of my inspection you are unreasonably denying me, and you claim there's nothing to hide? Is *that* what I must take back to the assembly with me and report to my colleagues? Shall I explain what my report is going to be to the *captain*?'

Silence. Cahill took a deep breath. Her previously perfect complexion was blotched. She sighed. 'Very well, Mister Assemblyman,' she said. 'Come along.'

8

As far as George Twill was concerned, no matter who upstairs won or lost, he himself was the luckiest person on this ship. He was fifty-one years of age, and he'd been more than two years out of a job, after the State Street in Albany branch of Merchants Bank downsized him. Twenty-two years of steady employment, and boom. Unemployment insurance gone, severance pay almost used up, savings dwindling, no jobs anywhere. Supermarket assistant manager; movie theater manager; parking garage manager; even motel desk clerk: every job went to somebody else. George was feeling pretty desperate by the time he joined the hundreds of other people who responded to the newspaper ad for jobs on this ship, to fill in for the people who hadn't traveled with it up from the south.

And he got the job. Teller in the money room, so here he was a teller again, though a very different kind of teller from before. But the people in the money room had to not only have some banking background but they also needed solid reputations, because they'd be bonded, so that was why George Twill was at last employed again, at better than his old salary at the bank. And *this* job wouldn't be taken over by an ATM machine.

He was by far the oldest of the five people who worked in here, probably twenty years older than his immediate boss, Pete Hancourt, whose job title was cashier but who was known in the room as Pete. They were a pretty informal bunch in here, happy in their work, and with one another. The two women were Helen and Ruth, and the other male teller was Sam. They worked day shift four days, then three days off, then night shift three nights, then four days off. Good pay, easy hours, fine co-workers; heaven, after the hell of the last two years.

The other thing George had, because he was the oldest here, was one extra responsibility. He was in charge of the panic button. It was on the floor, a large flat metal circle that stuck up no more than an inch, and it was an easy reach, maybe eighteen inches, from where his left foot was normally positioned when he was seated at his counter. If anything ever happened in here that wasn't supposed to happen, like a fire or a sudden illness or a leak in the side of the ship—all of them extremely unlikely—it would be George's job to reach over with his left foot and press down just once on that button. Otherwise, his responsibility was not to bump into that button inadvertently. No problem; it was tucked well out of the way.

The work here was easy and repetitive and he didn't mind it a bit. The vacuum canisters came down, with cash for chips, or chips for cash. George and the other three tellers made the transactions and kept track of the drawers of money and the drawers of chips. No cash was used up in the casino; even the slots took only chips.

At the beginning of each run, down here in the money room, they'd have a full supply of chips and just a little money. By the end of each run, they'd be down fifty or a hundred chips, because people forgot they had them in their pockets or wanted to keep them as souvenirs, and they would have a lot of money, particularly on Friday and Saturday nights. It was fascinating to see the efficiency with which it worked. And if George Twill had ever had a tendency toward being a betting man—which he had not—being around this efficient money machine would have cured it.

When the buzzer sounded, all of a sudden, at twenty minutes to one, it startled them all, and at first George had no idea what that sound was. Then he remembered; it was the bell for the door, the entry to and from the rest of the ship that was always kept locked and that none of them ever used. He'd only heard it once before, the third day of his employment, and that time it had been the ship's nurse, a recent hire like George, bringing around medical history forms to be filled out. Apparently, she hadn't realized she wasn't supposed to have done it that way, but mailed it to their homes. Pete said he'd heard that a couple of executives from the company had really reamed her out that time.

So whatever this was, it wouldn't be the nurse again. Feeling his responsibility, and feeling also a sudden nervousness, wondering what this would turn out to be, George moved his foot closer to the panic button and watched Pete, frowning deeply, walk over to the door and speak into the intercom there.

George could hear that it was a woman's voice that answered, but he couldn't make out the words. Pete said something else, the woman said something else, Pete said something else, and then Pete unlocked the door.

Susan Cahill came in. George remembered her, she was one of the people who'd interviewed him when he applied for the job. She'd seemed remote and cold and a little scary, and he'd thought she didn't like him and would recommend against his being hired, but apparently he'd been wrong. This was the first time he was seeing her since, and the familiar face eased his tension and brought his left foot back to its normal spot on the floor.

Three men followed Susan Cahill into the room. The first was short and stout and grumpy-looking, glaring around at everybody as though looking for the person who stole his wallet. The other two men were large—one of them huge—blank-faced, tough-looking, in dark suits and ties.

Susan Cahill said, 'Thank you, Pete,' then addressed the rest of the room. She seemed to George to be annoyed or upset about something, and trying to hide it. 'Ladies and gentlemen,' she said, 'this is Assemblyman Morton Kotkind, from the New York State legislature, and he's here on an inspection tour of the ship. We operate, as you know, at the discretion of the legislature. Assemblyman Kotkind wanted to see where the money eventually comes. These are his . . . aides, they are state troopers, Trooper Helsing and Trooper Renfield.'

'That's funny,' Pete said, grinning at the two troopers.

They turned and gave him blank looks that seemed to contain a hint of menace. Susan Cahill, sounding frazzled, said, 'What's funny?'

Pete seemed to belatedly realize this was a formal occasion, not a casual one. 'Nothing,' he said, and avoided the troopers' eyes as he turned to say to George and the others, 'Folks, just keep doing what you're doing. The congressman is here to see how the operation works.'

'Assemblyman,' the grumpy man said.

'Oh. Sorry.'

A vacuum canister slid into the basket in front of George. He picked it up, twisted it open, and five one-hundred-dollar bills dropped out, along with the upstairs cashier's transit slip. Only an hour left on the cruise, and they were still buying chips.

*   *   *

Grey Hanzen, in the darkness at the water's edge, stripped out of shoes and socks and pants. What he really wanted to do was get back in his car and drive down to the Kingston bridge and across the Hudson River and line out west and not stop until the water in front of him was the Pacific Ocean. If only.

How had he got himself into this mess? It had all been so simple and easy to begin with. Now there were all these different bunches of people, and him in the middle like a grain of wheat in a goddam mill. Any one of those people could crush him in a second, and most of them would have reason. How in the good Lord's name was he going to steer himself through these rapids and come out safe and alive on the other side?

'I should just get the hell out of here,' he told himself out loud as he waded into the cold water. Gloomy, despairing, not even pretending to have hope, he waded out to his boat, threw his clothing into the bottom and climbed in.

Nothing else to do. You can't escape your goddam fate, that's all.

*   *   *

He was certainly taking his time about it, this assemblyman. George found it hard to concentrate on the task at hand, the numbers coming in, the numbers going out, with those three silent men moving around and around the room, slowly pacing, stopping from time to time to watch a particular operation. They didn't ask any questions at all, which was a relief. But their presence was distracting and made the room feel uncomfortable.

Now the assemblyman was standing beside George, just to his right, watching George twist open a canister, make his entries into the computer terminal in front of him, slide the greenbacks into their bins in their drawer, put the transit slip in its bin, scoop out the right denomination of chips—

He was on the floor. He had no idea what happened, he just had a moment of disorientation and panic. Why am I on the floor? Heart attack?

He was on his right side on the floor, and the left side of his head felt a sharp stinging pain. He blinked, thinking he'd fallen, blacked out, and the pain spread across his head from that electric grinding point just above his left ear, and when he looked up, the bigger of the two state troopers was standing over him, but not looking at him, looking across him at the other people in the room, pointing at them, saying—

A gun. Pointing a gun. A pistol, a gun. Pointing a gun at the people in the room, saying, 'Hands on your desks. Helen, Ruth. Come on, Sam, you don't want to die.'

And another voice—the other trooper, it must be—was saying, 'Pete, hands on your head. Susan, if you reach for that beeper, you're dead.'

He hit me, George thought, and felt more astonishment at that than even at the fact of the gun and the things they were saying. We aren't children in a schoolyard, we don't hit each other, we don't—

It's a robbery.

The shock of it, being hit, being all at once on the floor, feeling such pain, seeing the astonishing sight of that gun in that man's hand, had befuddled George for so long that only now—thirty seconds? forty?—did he realize what this meant. These people were robbing the ship!

The big one, who'd hit him—with the side of that gun, it must be—now looked down at George. He didn't point the gun at him, but he didn't have to, not with those cold eyes. He said, 'George, you can sit up, cross your knees, put your hands on your knees. Don't reach a foot toward that button, George.'

He knows! They know everything, they know my *name*!

A sudden spasm of guilt washed through George, and he twisted around to stare toward

Pete and Susan Cahill. They'll think it's me! They'll think I'm the one told these people everything, and I'll lose my job, and I'll go to jail!

The assemblyman—no, he can't be an assemblyman, it's all a fake—he was frisking Pete, while the other non-trooper, also now holding a gun, was taking the beeper off Susan Cahill's belt. Pete looked frightened, but Susan Cahill was looking outraged. Both were too involved in what was happening to see George stare at them, so George quickly shifted to look at something else. Don't act guilty, he told himself. Don't make them suspect you.

Susan Cahill, her voice trembling with fury, suddenly spoke: 'This is outrageous! How *dare* you men, how *dare* you behave like this! The police will get you, the police will get you, and Avenue Resorts will be *very* tough, you can count on that!'

The non-trooper who'd taken her beeper ignored her, turning away to look at the non-trooper standing over George. 'Tape,' he said, and pocketed his gun.

'Sure.'

This one reached inside his jacket and took out a compact roll of duct tape. He tossed it across to the other one, then looked down and said, 'George, I told you to sit *up.*'

'Yes. Yes. All right.' He didn't want to be hit again, or whatever worse might happen. He scrambled into a seated position, making

185

a point of moving away from that button, that he could *see* just over there, under the counter. But no power on Earth would make him move toward that button, not even to save his job.

The non-trooper with Susan Cahill peeled off some tape and said to her, 'Hands behind your back.'

'I certainly will *not!*' She folded her arms under her breasts and glared. 'If you think you'll get *away* with—'

He slapped her, left-handed, open-handed, but hard, the sound almost like a baseball being hit by a bat. All of them in the room jumped at the sound, George and Pete and Helen and Ruth and Sam. The three robbers didn't jump.

Susan Cahill staggered from the slap, and stared at the non-trooper, who stepped closer to her and said, as though he really wanted to know the answer, 'Are those your teeth?'

She gaped at him. 'What?'

'Are *those* your teeth?'

She didn't know the reason for the question, but she was suddenly afraid not to answer. 'Yes.'

'Do you want to keep them?'

This answer was smaller, more defeated. 'Yes.'

'Hands behind your back.'

She put her hands behind her back, quivering now with fear, but George could tell that the outrage and the fury were still there inside her, merely prudently banked for the moment. The non-trooper duct-taped her wrists, then started to put another piece of duct tape over her mouth, but she pulled her head away. He stopped, and looked at her, and the next time he moved the duct tape she didn't resist. As he put it over her mouth, he said, 'If I was a bad guy, or if you irritated me, I'd put this over your nose, too. You're going to sit down now.' He took her arm to help her, and she sat on the floor, and he duct-taped her ankles together.

Meantime, the fake assemblyman had been ordering the others around, telling Helen and Ruth and Sam—by name—to keep doing what they were doing, handling the money and the chips, and not to vary the routine in any way. For instance, not to send anything more or less than normal up to the cashier's cage in each vacuum canister.

'I'll tell you why,' he said. 'It isn't your money, and it would be stupid to die for it. The line's insured, you'll still get your salary. If there's trouble, we may get caught but you will absolutely certainly get dead. So cooperate, and this little unpleasantness will soon be over. Pete?'

Pete jumped again, as when Susan Cahill was slapped. 'Yes? What?'

'Easy, Pete, gentle down, there's a love. And here's a plastic bag. I want you to fill it with the cash from George's station, since he won't

187

be working any more tonight.'

'All right.'

As Pete came over with the white plastic bag—kitchen can size—the one non-trooper finished with Susan Cahill and tossed the duct tape back to the one by George, who said, 'Okay, George, your turn. Hands behind your back.' And, as he put his gun in his pocket, the other one across the room took his out again.

George said, 'Excuse me, I'm sorry, but I—'

'Come on, George.'

No long explanations, not with these people; only short explanations. George blurted out, 'I have asthma!'

The big man looked at him. He seemed really interested. 'Yeah? Had it long?'

George hadn't expected that question. He said, 'Fifteen years. And—I can't always breathe through my nose, I'm afraid, if you put that tape on—'

'I get it, George,' the big man said. 'If you got asthma real bad like that, you probably carry some kind of medicine for it, am I right? An inhaler, something like that?'

'Yes.'

'How slow can you take it out of your pocket, George?'

'Very slow.'

'Go ahead.'

George kept his inhaler in his inside jacket pocket, and now realized that was exactly where a tough guy or a bad guy would keep a gun. Hand trembling, sweat starting to trickle down his face, breath becoming raspy already, he reached into his pocket, grasped the inhaler, lost it through his trembling fingers, grasped it again, jerked his hand back, shuddered the motion to a stop, and slowly and shakily brought the little tube into sight.

The big man seemed pleased. 'Good, George,' he said. 'Now, if you gave yourself a spray or two with that, you'd be okay for a while, wouldn't you?'

'I think so,' George said.

'We both think so, George,' the big man said. 'Go ahead, take a shot.'

George did. He had so much trouble keeping his right hand steady that he held it with the left hand so he could fit the inhaler into his mouth, lips closed over it, and direct the spray at the back of his throat. He did this twice, and while he did the big man said to the other one, 'There's a lot of asthma around these days, you know? Worse than ever. It comes from mold, a lot of times, and I read someplace, you can get it from cockroach dander. Can you believe it? You try to keep yourself in shape and some fucking cockroach is out to bring you down. You set, George?'

George put the inhaler back in his pocket. 'Yes.'

Hunkered beside him, applying the duct tape, the big man in a friendly manner said, 'What I think you should do, now that the

189

working day is done, you got time on your hands, I think you should spend it working on what you're gonna say to the TV news reporters.'

*   *   *

'And now, in sports—'

Hilliard Cathman sighed in exasperation; mostly with himself. He knew he should turn off this 'news-radio' station, which was in truth mostly a sports-score-and-advertising radio station, and go to sleep, but lately he was having even more trouble than usual dropping off, and he had this need to know, to know when they did it. He had to know.

It would be a weekend, that much was certain, when the ship would be the most full of gamblers, when the most money would be lost. A Friday or a Saturday night, and soon. Possibly even tonight.

Wouldn't that be wonderful? Tonight. Get it over with, get this tension behind him at last.

He knew the risk he was taking, the danger he was in. Sitting up in bed past midnight, lights on in half the house, the nightstand radio eagerly rattling off the endless results of games he cared nothing about, Cathman reminded himself he'd known from the beginning the perils in this idea, but had decided the goal was worth it. And it was, and it still was, though these days all Cathman could really see was the expression in that man Parker's eyes. Which was no expression at all.

Marshall Howell had been different, easier to work with, easier to believe one could win out against. He'd been a tough man, and a criminal, but with some humanity in him. This one, Parker . . .

It will happen, that's all, and I don't need to know about it the instant it does. When it happens, I'll know soon enough, and then one of three things will happen. Parker will come bring me my ten per cent, which is the least likely, and I'll deal with him in the way I'm ready to deal with him. Or he and the rest of them will fade away, and I have his telephone number, and from that I have found his house, and I have seen his wife, none of which he knows, and I can finish it the other way. Or they will get caught, which would be the best thing, and I will be ready for that as well.

'The time is twelve fifty-two. In tomorrow's weather—'

Oh, enough. Cathman reached out and switched off the radio, but left the lights on. He lay on his back and stared at the ceiling, and for a long time he didn't sleep.

*　　　*　　　*

Only Ruth was still at her station at the counter, dealing with vacuum canisters as they came down from the cashier's cage upstairs.

191

George could see the others, Pete and Helen and Sam and Susan Cahill, all seated like him on the floor, backs against the wall, duct-taped into silence and immobility. A degree of background panic gave his own breathing a level of fibrillation that scared him some, but he knew it was under control, that unless something else happened he'd be able to go on breathing through to the end of this.

What was coming down now, from the cashier's cage, at nearly one o'clock in the morning, was mostly chips being cashed in, and very rarely a purchase of more chips by some diehard loser up above. There wasn't much activity at all at this point, and it really would be sensible for the robbers to get out of here now, before they lost part of their loot to customers upstairs cashing in, which they seemed to realize. George watched them give one another little looks and nods and hand signals, and then the one who'd slapped Susan Cahill went over and opened the door, the door they'd come through that was never opened—and how much better if it never had been opened—and headed up the stairs.

George knew there was a guard on duty up there, though he'd never seen him, seated at a desk on the landing in front of the door at the top of the stairs. That guard would have seen this robber with Susan Cahill when they came down, he wouldn't suspect a thing, somebody coming up the stairs like that, he'd been hired to keep people from going *down* those stairs.

Yes. Here he came, a beefy young man in a tan uniform, looking bewildered and angry and scared, hands knitted on top of his uniform hat on his head, holster at his right side hanging empty, the robber now holding two guns, one in each hand, shutting the door with his heel as he came in.

The big one, the one who'd taped George, went smiling over to the guard, saying 'Welcome aboard, Jack. You are Jack, aren't you?'

The guard stared at all the trussed people. He stared at the big man. He burst out, 'Jesus, you're not supposed to *do* this!'

The big man laughed. 'Oh, I know,' he said. 'We're just regular scamps. Put your hands behind your back, Jack.' Then he laughed again and said to the one with the two guns in his hands, 'Back, Jack; how do you like that?' To the guard he said, 'I'm so glad your name isn't Tim I'm not even gonna punch you in the belly for not having your hands behind your back. Not yet, I'm not.'

The guard quickly moved his arms, like a panicky drowner lunging toward the surface, and when his hands were behind his back the big man duct-taped them, then his mouth, then helped him sit, then did his ankles.

During which George watched the man who'd claimed to be an assemblyman, but who now seemed much more believable as an

193

armed robber, take a small screwdriver from his pocket and use it to open the control box next to the outer door, the door in the hull through which George and the others would exit at the end of their shift, through which the money would be carried into the armored car, and George saw that what he was doing was dismantling the alarm system in there. Supposedly, if this door were to be opened while the ship was in motion, an alarm would ring up on the bridge; but not now.

Surprised, George thought, why, they've planned it all out.

*   *   *

Carlow pushed Noelle's wheelchair into the elevator. The four other people in the car smiled at her, and she smiled wanly back, and the tiredness she showed was probably real. Carlow felt the same way; this was the longest night of all.

When the elevator doors opened, one level down, the other four people dispersed themselves into the restrooms, the couple who'd been waiting here boarded the elevator—after a smile at wan Noelle—and Carlow pushed the wheelchair over to the door that led to the stairs down to the money room. It was a discreet door, painted to blend with the wall around it. Carlow turned the wheelchair around to face out, then rapped

194

the door once with his heel.

The door opened inward. Carlow heard the click, and immediately went down to one knee. He grasped the handle of the box beneath the seat and pulled out a very different box from the one in the other wheelchair. This one was deeper and wider and much longer, and contained no bowl, empty or full. Carlow slid the box backward, looking down, and saw Parker's hand grab it. Carlow stood, and the door behind him clicked shut.

They stood there for three minutes. A few people passed, and all smiled at Noelle, but all kept going. Everybody was tired, and they knew she must be tired, too, so they left her alone.

A knock sounded on the door behind him. Two couples, yawning together, waited for the elevator. He watched them, and then the elevator came, empty this time, and they boarded, and its doors shut.

Then Carlow rapped the door with his heel again, and went to one knee, and the box was slid out to him. It was much heavier now, filled with white plastic bags. Carlow slid it into place, stood, pushed the wheelchair over to the elevator, boarded it the next time it arrived.

*　　　*　　　*

The money usually went into heavy canvas sacks to be carried off the ship, and the robbers had thoughtfully cut air holes into these sacks before putting them over everybody's head, but had then made sure the airholes weren't placed so the people could see through them.

What don't they want us to see, George wondered. There was a faint smell inside the money sack, not of money, but of something like a cabin in the woods or a thatched hut. The smell made George fearful again of his ability to breathe, but he kept himself from giving way to panic, and he breathed slowly and steadily through his nose, and he told himself he was going to survive, he was going to survive.

It wasn't the TV news reporters' questions he was thinking about now, it was the questions the police would ask. He'd be able to give full descriptions of the robbers, and he'd be able to describe just about everything they did and said.

And now there was the question of what the robbers didn't want them to see. All he had left now was his ears, and he listened as hard as he could. He heard shuffling noises, and then he heard a click of some kind, and wondered what that was. There was something familiar about that click, and yet there wasn't. Inside the canvas sack, George frowned deeply, breathing automatically, not even thinking about his breath now, and tried to think what that click could be, what it reminded him of, where he'd heard it before.

He almost got it, he was seconds from understanding, when another sound distracted him. A whoosh and a foamy rush, and a sudden sense of cool damp air, a breeze wafting over him.

They'd opened the outer door. *That* must be what they didn't want him and the others to see; what sort of transportation awaited them outside.

George strained to hear, leaning forward, staring at the canvas a half inch from his eyes. He heard murmuring, vague movement, and then not even that. And then a slam, as the outer door was shut again.

They've gone, he thought, and never did remember that click any more, and so didn't come to the memory that would have told him that the click was the sound of the inner door closing. And so he never did get to tell the police the one thing they would have been interested to hear: that before the robbers left, one of them went upstairs.

*   *   *

Greg Hanzen trailed the big gleaming ship for several miles, and at every second he wanted to veer off, run for his life. But he was afraid to leave them stranded there, afraid they'd escape anyway somehow and come after him. They would surely come after him.

They might anyway.

The door in the side of the ship, up ahead of him, opened inward, showing a vertical oval of light. Immediately, not permitting himself to think, Hanzen drove forward, in close to the ship's flank, up along the side of that open doorway, where Parker stood in the light, empty-handed.

Hanzen tossed him the line, and Parker handed it on to a much bigger man, who stood grinning down at Hanzen as he held Hanzen's little boat firm against the *Spirit of the Hudson* while Parker and a third man jumped in. Then the big man grabbed the outer handle of the door and jumped across into the boat, slamming the door behind him. That would be, Hanzen guessed, so that there wouldn't be an unexpected light in the hull of the boat for the next hour, to maybe draw attention from shore.

'Okay,' Parker said.

But something was wrong. Hanzen looked at the three of them. 'Where's the money?'

Parker said, 'That's going a different way.'

Oh, Christ. Oh, what a fuckup. Hanzen had an instant of even worse despair than usual, and then, afraid Parker might see something on his face, he turned away to the wheel and said, 'Well, let's get us out of here.'

He put on speed and veered away from the ship into the darkness, as they opened the duffel bag Parker had given him earlier to bring along on the boat. Here were the clothes they would change into, to become fishermen out at night, while the suits and ties and white shirts, into the duffel bag with a rock, would soon be resting on the river bottom.

Hanzen gritted his teeth and chewed his lower lip. Had he given himself away? He snuck a look at Parker, and the man was frowning at him, thinking it over.

Oh, Jesus, I did! He saw it! He knows already. Oh, Christ, *everybody's* got a reason to be down on poor Greg Hanzen, and I never wanted any of it. Low man on the totem pole again. Why didn't I cut and run when I could?

Whoever survives this night, Hanzen told himself, if anybody does, it won't be me.

9

One-fifteen. It wasn't necessary for Noelle to pitch her faint for another fifteen or twenty minutes, but she was ready to do it now. She really did feel queasy as hell, and it wasn't because she was on a ship; the motion of the *Spirit of the Hudson* as it coursed upstream was barely noticeable.

No, and it wasn't the money under her that had her queasy, either. She understood about that, and agreed with the thinking behind it, and had no trouble with it. She'd been the girl distraction more than once in her life, either carrying the dangerous stuff herself or fronting for the one who did, though she'd never done it as an invalid before. But the idea here was a good one; she was an established presence on the ship. The robbers would have left through the door in the hull, and why wouldn't they have taken the money with them?

Of course, the reason they hadn't taken the money with them was because they would be half an hour or more in that small boat on the river before they reached the safety of the cabin. Nobody knew how soon the alarm would be raised, but when it was, there would be police boats out. They might be suspicious of four night fishermen, but on that boat they wouldn't find any guns, any dress clothes, and most importantly, no money.

Would the police have any reason to think the money was still on the ship? None. Why would they believe that three men would go through such an elaborate con job and robbery and then not take the money with them?

So Noelle wasn't worried about being caught sitting on several hundred thousand dollars. What had her shaky and nauseous was something much simpler; she was dehydrated. Having to sit for over six hours every night in this damn wheelchair—or the other wheelchair, actually, up till tonight—without any opportunity to leave it for any reason at all, meant she'd been avoiding liquids as much as possible the last eight days.

Six hours without a bathroom isn't easy, if you stay with a normal intake of liquids, so Noelle had been cutting back, and finding it a little chancy anyway, and by tonight the drying-out had begun to affect her. She knew it already in the van driving up to Albany, but she didn't dare do anything about it then, with the whole night in front of her, so she'd been hanging in there, feeling sicker and sicker, until by now what she was most afraid of was dry heaves; and dry they'd be.

Apart from the physical discomfort, though, she was having no trouble with this job. Since she and Tommy had split up, it had been harder to find strings to attach to, so money had often been a problem, which tonight should go a long way to solve.

And another good thing about this crowd was, none of them felt he had to hit on her. Parker had his woman Claire, and the other three all seemed to understand that she was simply another member of the crew, and it would screw things up entirely if they got out of line. Also, they probably knew she could be difficult if annoyed; they might even have heard about the guy she'd kneecapped in St Louis.

It would probably be better all around if she found some other guy on the bend to hook up with, but she'd gotten along before Tommy and she'd get along now, and if another guy appeared, fine. It would certainly be easier, though, if Uncle Ray were still alive.

It was her father's older brother, Ray Braselle, a heister from way back, who'd brought her into the game, over her pharmacist father's objections. Ray Braselle had been around for so long that once, in describing the first bank job he was ever on, he'd said, 'And I stood on the running board,' and then he'd had to explain what a running board was.

Uncle Ray was all right, though old as the goddam hills. But the people he ran with were more like Parker; tough, but not just smash-and-grab, always with a plan, a contingency, ways in and ways out. For guys like that, a good-looking girl could frequently be part of the plan, and if she was a pro herself, steady and reliable, not a hooker and not a junkie, who knew how to handle a gun, an alarm system or a cop, so much the better.

Uncle Ray liked to spend his free time living off away by himself, in a scrubby ranch he had in Wyoming, north of Cheyenne, up in the foothills before the high mountains toward Montana, and it was there that a horse rolled on him—some kind of accident, no way to be sure exactly what happened—and the body wasn't found for six days. After that, Noelle still got the occasional call from guys she and Ray had worked with, and on one of those jobs she'd met Tommy Carpenter, and they'd lived together for a few years until all of a sudden it turned out Tommy was afraid of the law, so here she was on her own. And feeling mighty sick.

Should she ask Mike to get her a glass of water? No; the very idea made her feel even worse. What would happen if she tried to drink water and she threw it up, right here in this chair? Down to the nurse's office, no way to avoid it; the change of clothing, the examination, the discovery of the money; ten to fifteen in a prison laundry.

Hang in there, she told herself, and to Mike she said, 'Mike, could we stay in one place for a while? I feel like shit.'

'I thought you did,' he said. 'Before you start feeling better, let's go talk to the purser.'

'Good.'

They'd done this on two other nights, so the purser would be used to the idea. Half an hour or so before the ship would dock, they'd go to the purser and Mike would quietly explain that Jane Ann was feeling kind of bad, a little worse than usual, and would it be okay if they got off first, the instant the ship was made fast? Hey, no problem. No problem twice before this, and it should be no problem tonight.

Getting to the purser's office meant another elevator ride; Noelle gulped a lot, and breathed through her mouth, and held tight to the wheelchair arms, and didn't at all have to put on an act for the other people in the elevator.

The purser's office was open on one side, to an interior lobby, with a chest-high counter. The purser himself was there, with two of his girl assistants, all three of them in the blue and gold uniforms. He wanted them to call him Jerry, and he gave them a big smile as they approached: 'Hey, Mike. How you doin', Jane Ann? Enjoyin' the ride?' Nobody ever asked anybody if they were winning or losing; that was considered bad taste.

'Not so much, Jerry,' Noelle told him, and swallowed hard.

Jerry looked stricken, as though he thought the ship was to blame, and Mike leaned close to him to say, 'I hate to be a pest, Jerry, asking special favors all the time—' as the phone on the desk behind the counter rang and one of the girls answered it.

'Hey, no problem, Mike,' Jerry said. 'I can see Jane Ann's ready to call it a day. You bed down in that lounge again, you remember? and— Excuse me.'

Because the girl who'd answered the phone wanted to say a quick word to Jerry, who tilted his head toward her while continuing to face Mike and Noelle.

One strange thing about all these hours in the wheelchair was the way it changed your perspective on everybody else. They were all big people now, and she was little. Seated in the wheelchair, she was too low to actually see

204

the countertop, but could look at an angle up past it at the faces of Jerry and his girl assistant as the girl, in low tones that nevertheless Noelle could hear, said, 'The cashier's cage say they're not getting any change.'

Jerry looked blank, but continued to smile at Mike and Noelle. He said, 'What?'

'People want to cash in now,' she told him, 'and they're sending down the chips, but nothing's coming back up.'

Here we go, Noelle thought. One twenty-seven by the big clock on the wall at the back of the purser's office. Here's where the hairy part begins. Sooner or later, cops are going to come aboard, and they're going to want to know if there are any anomalies here tonight, any odd or unusual passengers, and will they look at a girl in a wheelchair? Sooner or later they might, but not if she's long gone, off and away from here.

'Excuse me,' Jerry said, and turned away from them, and made a quick phone call. Four numbers; internal. Calling the money room. Waiting. Listening. Waiting. Looking confused.

Exactly one-thirty. Jerry hung up, and stood still for a second, frowning this way and that, trying to decide what to do. Mike said, 'Jerry? Something wrong?'

'No, no,' Jerry said. 'Just a little, uh, communication problem. Excuse me, one second.' He made another internal call, and

205

this time it was answered right away, and he said, 'It's Jerry. We're not getting anything up from the money room, and when I called down there there's no answer. Can you beep your guy at the top of the stairs? Well, can you send somebody over, see what's up? Thanks, Doug.'

Mike, sounding worried, said, 'Jerry? Is there gonna be a problem?'

'I'm sure there isn't,' Jerry promised him. 'Maybe there's an electric failure down there, who knows what. They'll take a look.'

Mike, more confidential than ever, said, 'Jerry, the reason—See, I'm responsible for Jane Ann.'

'I know, Mike, and you do a great—'

'Yeah, but, see, if there's gonna be a problem— Jerry, I gotta get this girl home.'

'Don't you worry, Mike, we'll get Jane Ann home, there isn't going to be any reason not. You've got my word on this, okay?'

'Would it be okay,' Mike asked, 'if we stuck around here to find out what's going on? You know, just so we know. I mean, if we gotta get the medevac helicopter, we oughta know that right—'

Jerry blanched, but rallied. 'If it comes to that,' he said, 'we'll move fast, don't you worry, but it isn't gonna come to that. Sure, stick around, I'm happy to have the company. Jane Ann? Anything I can get you?'

'Oh, no,' she said, and put a trembling hand over her mouth.

Jerry looked as though he couldn't figure out which of his problems he should worry about most.

*   *   *

One thirty-three by the big clock, and the phone rang. The same girl assistant answered, then said to Jerry, 'Doug.'

'Right. Jerry here. Yeah? *What?* Holy *shit*, I—I—I mean *hell*! *Jesus*! What are we— Yeah, okay, I'll come up, too, who knows *what* the fuck we're supposed—oh, God. I'll come up.'

He slammed the phone down and gave Noelle an agonized look, saying, 'I *do* apologize, Jane Ann, I'm very sorry, that isn't like me, to use language like—I was just—I'm overwhelmed.'

Mike said, 'Jerry? What is it?'

'I've gotta go see the captain.' Jerry was well and truly rattled.

Mike said, 'Jerry, don't leave us like this. What's going on?'

Jerry looked both ways, then leaned over the counter and gave them a harsh stage whisper: 'We've been robbed!'

'What?' Mike was as astonished as Jerry. 'You're kidding me, nobody could—' Then, moving as though prepared to fling himself between Noelle and an approaching bullet, he said, 'They're on the ship? You've got robbers on—'

207

'No, no, they—I don't know, apparently they came in through the door in the hull, there's a separate door there, I don't know if you ever noticed, the armored car, at the dock—'

'No,' Mike said. 'They came in through some door in the hull? The side of the ship, you mean?'

'And I guess back out again,' Jerry said. 'With the money.'

Noelle said, 'Jerry?'

He leaned close to give her a solicitous look, and to say, 'Don't worry Jane Ann, we'll still get you off, just as *soon* as we dock.'

'Thank you, Jerry,' she said, 'but that's not what I wanted to say. Jerry, do you realize what this is? It's piracy!'

Jerry reared back, thinking about that. 'By golly you're right,' he said.

Noelle said, 'Look for a man with an eye patch.' And, despite how miserable she felt, she smiled.

*　　　*　　　*

At one forty-five they made the announcement over the loudspeaker. The money room had been robbed by gunmen who escaped in a small boat. More money was coming from the bank and would meet the boat, and people who still had chips to turn in would be able to do so while exiting the ship. There would be two exit ramps, so if you didn't want to cash in any chips you wouldn't have to wait on that line. All passengers would be required to give their names and addresses and show identification to the police when debarking, but otherwise would not be detained. The ship, its crew and its owners apologized for any inconvenience.

The ship was abuzz with excitement and rumor, and Mike and Noelle stayed well away from it. Mike asked permission to stay in the purser's office till they landed, to protect Jane Ann, and the distracted Jerry agreed, but they didn't hear any more about what was going on. The action had apparently moved to the security office.

When at last they docked in Albany, Jerry was as good as his word. He personally escorted them to the lounge near the exit, he spoke to the first police officers who boarded, and there was no problem about departure from the ship.

Mike showed his fake chauffeur's ID, gave Jane Ann Livingston's spurious address in a mansion on the Hudson, and three minutes after the ship had tied up at the dock he was pushing a thoroughly beat-up Noelle down the gangplank and through the departure building and out to the parking lot, where for the last time he did the elaborate ramp arrangement that got her wheelchair into the van. Then he got behind the wheel, and drove them away

209

from there.

The second traffic light they hit was red, and while stopped he looked at her in his inside mirror and said, 'How you doing?'

'Ask me,' she told him, 'three beers from now.'

10

Ray Becker woke up. Holy shit, he fell asleep!

Around ten he'd driven away from the cottages and down into a nearby town to a pizza place, where he got a small pizza and a can of Coke, and came back, and sat here on the porch in the dark, looking out at the black river, with the living room and kitchen lights on in the cabin behind him, and while he ate he thought about where he'd go, once he had his hands on the money.

He wished he could just get completely out of the United States, but he didn't dare. He wasn't sure he could cross any border without ID, and he didn't have any ID he'd care to show anybody official. And if he went somewhere else in the world, what would he know about the place? The laws, the systems, the ways things worked. What would he know about how they handled things? He'd be crippling himself, that's all, and for what?

No, he'd have to stay in the States, which

210

meant he'd have to go somewhere that was both out of the way and far from home; he wouldn't want to run into any old high school pals on the street.

But it couldn't be just anywhere. There were states, for instance, like Florida and Louisiana, that had a floating population of petty crooks and therefore had a lot of police forces alert to the idea of checking out any strangers who hung around too long. For similar reasons, big cities like New York and Chicago were out; but they were out anyway, because Becker had never felt comfortable in big cities.

He'd thought about Oregon and he'd thought about Maine, but the idea of the weather in both those places daunted him. On the other hand, if he went too far south, he'd stand out too much.

Maybe some place like Colorado or Kansas. Move in to some medium-size town, just settle in for a while, then get fresh ID, invest some of the money in a local business, start a new life.

ID wouldn't be a problem, he knew how to do that. You'd choose a good-sized city— Omaha, say, or St Louis—and look in the newspaper obits there for the year you were born, where you'd eventually find a child that had died before its second birthday. Using that child's name, you'd write to the Hall of Records in that city to ask for a copy of your birth certificate. Using that, you'd go to the nearest Social Security office and explain you'd

211

lived outside the US since you were a kid, with your parents, but now you were back and you needed to sign up. With those two pieces of ID, and the same off-shore story, you'd go get your driver's license, and all of a sudden you were as legit as any citizen in the country.

Kansas, he thought, that's where I'll go, check it out, see if that's the place for me, and on that thought he'd fallen asleep.

Only to spring awake, with the realization that he'd almost made a huge mistake. A *huge* mistake. If the robbers came back with the money and Ray Becker was sprawled in this chair asleep, that would be it. No questions. No more chances.

Kansas? Bottom of the Hudson River, more likely.

The lights are still on! What time is it?

He was trying to look at his watch and jump up from the Adirondack chair, both at the same time, when a voice said, 'Whadaya suppose they left the lights on for?'

Becker froze. Someone in the kitchen, directly behind him. He stared ahead of himself, out at the blackness that contained the river, and he listened very hard to the space behind him.

A second voice: 'Maybe so they could find the place from the river.' Younger, more nasal, than the first voice.

'We'll leave it the way they left it,' said a third voice, older and heavier and beerier, like the first one. And how the fuck many of them *were* there? 'We want those boys walkin' in here all fat and sassy.'

Now he knew why he'd come awake. He must have heard them arrive somehow, a car door slamming or the front door opening or whatever it was.

Get off the porch; that's the first thing. Slowly and silently, without attracting attention, get off this goddam porch.

Becker eased forward off the Adirondack chair on to his hands and knees. Behind him they were talking, making themselves at home, opening and closing the refrigerator door. A beer can popped.

The screen door off this screened-in porch was ahead and to the right, and it opened inward. Becker crawled over there, found the door by feel, pulled it a little way open, and for a wonder it didn't squeak. Holding the door with his left hand, he shifted around to a seated position, then slid himself forward on his rump into the doorway, until his feet found the log step out there between porch level and the ground.

Easing himself out, and down on to that step, without letting the door slam, was damn tricky, but he did it, holding his hand between door and frame at the last, until he could get his feet under him, and reach up to the knob. He pushed the door open just a bit to free his hand, then eased it shut.

213

Darkness outside, with canyons of light vaulted from the windows. Becker eased along next to the building, peeked in the kitchen window, and saw three of them, all now with beers in their hands.

Bikers. Two big old rogue elephants, bearded and ponytailed and big-gutted, and one young ferret, all three of them in the black leather those boys like so much. One of them was the leader, and was telling the other two where to position themselves for the ambush to come; this one in this room, that one in that room.

Becker went back to the side of the porch, away from the light, then hurried around the next-door cottage to his pickup truck. From there he could see, gleaming in the living room light over there, three big motorcycles. So that's what had waked him, those hogs driving in. Damn good thing.

When he'd first rented the pickup, he'd removed the interior light, so it stayed dark when he gently opened the passenger door. There was a narrow storage space behind the bench-type seat, that you got to by tilting the seatback forward. Not much room back there, but enough for the shotgun he'd taken from the trunk of his patrol car when he'd ditched it, and also for the two handguns he'd always carried; his official sidearm, a Smith & Wesson Model 39, a 9 mm automatic with an eight-shot clip, and his extra, a little Smith &

Wesson .38 Chiefs Special, a very concealable revolver with a two-inch barrel.

For present purposes, he left the automatic, pocketed the revolver in case he needed to do in-close work, and headed back for the lit-up cottage, carrying the shotgun at port arms.

And now at last he looked at his watch: five minutes to two! Jesus Christ, they'll be back any minute! He had to get rid of those people, he had to get those lights switched off.

It's getting complicated again, goddam it, it's getting screwed-up again. Get it under control. Don't let things spin away into disaster like every other time, this is the last chance, the last chance. The last chance.

The leader first. Moving cautiously along, stooped to stay under the shafts of light, Becker found him in the bedroom off the kitchen, in semi-darkness, looking through the mostly shut doorway at the kitchen, patiently waiting. He had a beer can in his left hand, a big automatic in his right, like the one Becker had left in the truck.

Take care of this now. Take care of it all right now. Get it simple again.

Becker rested the tip of the barrel of the shotgun against the wood frame at the bottom of the screen over the window. The window was open, so it was only the screen in the way. Focusing past it, not seeing the screen at all when he did, Becker aimed the shotgun carefully at the center of the back of that head, just at the knot in the ponytail. His finger slowly squeezed down on the trigger.

FOUR

1

'We didn't leave lights on,' Parker said, and a shot sounded from up there, on shore.

He had both guns in his hands, the one he'd carried on to the ship in a shoulder holster and the one he'd taken from the guard on the stairs, because he'd planned to throw them out into the river as they left the boat, but now he turned and put the barrel of the Colt Python against Hanzen's near temple. 'Turn us around,' he said, being very quiet, because sound travels on water. 'Take us out of here.'

Hanzen did it, without an argument, without a reaction at all, as though he'd been expecting this.

'You know,' Wycza said, speaking as quietly as Parker had, 'I *thought* this thing was going along too easy.'

Parker said, 'We'll head for your landing.'

'Oh, shit,' Hanzen said, but that was all. Behind them, a second shot sounded, and in quick succession a third.

Parker hadn't one hundred per cent trusted Hanzen, but had felt he could take care of things if a problem came up. But why would people be shooting back there? Had they been shooting at this boat? What would be the purpose in that?

Nobody spoke for a good three minutes, as Hanzen steered them at a downstream angle out toward the middle of the river. They'd come from upstream, and Hanzen's landing was further on down. For those silent three minutes, Parker held the barrel of the Python against Hanzen's temple, and Hanzen hunched grimly over his wheel, looking straight ahead, asking nothing, offering nothing.

Finally, Parker tapped Hanzen's head lightly with the gun barrel. 'I can't hear you,' he said.

'You know the story,' Hanzen said. He sounded bitter.

'Not all of it.'

'Shit, man, *I* don't know *all* of it. Who's shooting back there? Beats the shit out of me. Maybe they got stoned, they're shooting at little green men. Wouldn't put it past them.'

That was possible. Or there could be more players in the game. Parker said, 'Just how many people you told my business?'

'Only them as leaned on me,' Hanzen said, 'and you met them.'

'They didn't buy our restaurant story, is that it?'

'A businessman don't offer to run over one of them's bikes. You come on too hard, so they wanted to know about you. I figure it's your way, you can't help it.'

Wycza said, 'What have we got, exactly?'

218

'Three bikers,' Parker told him. 'Friends of Hanzen.'

'Not friends,' Hanzen said.

'They do drug deals together,' Parker said. 'They saw me one time, I was with Hanzen, the story was I was looking for a site for a waterfront restaurant. Seems they didn't buy it, and they got curious.'

'They leaned on me,' Hanzen insisted, 'like I said.'

Wycza told him, 'I look at you, friend, it don't seem to me you'd need much leanin'l To Parker, he said, 'So Hanzen here told these biker friends of his where they could expect to find us with some money on us.'

'And went there first,' Parker said.

Lou Sternberg had been silent all this time, seated on the bottom of the boat because his balance wasn't good enough to permit him to stand when it was running through the water. But now he said, 'Parker, why are you still talking to this clown? This is a deep enough river, isn't it?'

'We couldn't find his landing on our own,' Parker said. Hanzen said, 'That's right, and we all know it. I'll take you to my place—you probably want my car.'

'Naturally.'

'So there it is,' Hanzen said. 'I'll take you there, you'll go ashore, you'll kill me, you'll take my car, my problems'll be all over and yours'll still be goin on.'

219

'Maybe not,' Parker said. 'You're cooperating, and you didn't tell them till they made you.'

'Don't try to give me hope,' Hanzen said, 'it's a waste of time.'

Which was probably true, too, so Parker didn't lie to him anymore.

'Leaned on him,' Wycza said, scoffing. 'They leaned on him. Made faces and said boo.'

'That's right,' Hanzen said, 'they did that, too. They also kicked me in the nuts a couple times, kicked me in the shins so I got some red scars you could look at, twisted my arms around fill I thought they broke 'em, closed a couple hands down on my windpipe till I passed out.' He turned away from the wheel, though still holding on to it, and looked Wycza up and down. 'You're a big guy,' he said, 'so you figure it don't happen to you. The day it does, big man, when you got seven or eight comin' at you, not to kill you but just to make you hurt, you remember Greg Hanzen.'

'I'll do that,' Wycza promised.

'And remember I told you this. They got wonderful powers of concentration, those boys, they never forget what they're doing. They don't stop. They won't stop, no matter how long it takes, until you say what they want you to say.'

'I'll remember that, too,' Wycza said.

'Good.' Hanzen turned back to the wheel. 'We're coming in now,' he said, and angled them toward shore.

It was still possible that Hanzen had some other scheme in mind, so Parker kept both guns in his hands and peered at the black and featureless shore as the boat slowed and the river grew wider behind them. How could these river rats find their way around in the dark like this? And yet they could.

'I'll run it on up on the shore,' Hanzen said. 'Make it easier for you all to get out.'

'Good,' Parker said.

Hanzen said, 'I hope you take them, and not the other way around. Them's the bunch I got a grudge against.'

'We'll do what we can,' Parker said.

Now the shore was close, very close. There was a little moon, not much, just enough to glint off glass in there; probably the windshield of Hanzen's car. Parker said, 'Where are the car keys?'

'In my pocket. Wait'll we stop.'

'Fine.'

'Brace yourselves now.'

Hanzen switched off the engine. There was a sudden tingling floating silence, and then the keel of the boat scraped pebbles in the mud, angled up, ran partway up on to the bank, and jolted to a stop. Hanzen reached into his pocket, came out with a small ring of keys, and extended them toward Parker, who took them. 'It pulls to the left,' Hanzen said.

Wycza stepped over the side first on to the

bank, then helped Lou Sternberg over. Parker jumped over the side, and Hanzen jumped after him. Then Hanzen stood there, just waiting.

Wycza took Hanzen by the elbow, walked him farther from the water's edge, into the oval clearing, very dark now. They stopped, and Wycza stepped to one side. He said, 'Greg.'

Hanzen turned his head, and Wycza clipped him across the jaw with a straight right. Hanzen dropped like a puppet when you cut the strings; straight down.

Wycza turned to the others. 'Okay, let's go,' he said. 'I see it's another goddam tiny car. Lou, you're in back.'

Sternberg said, 'Dan, he isn't dead.'

'Oh, what the fuck,' Wycza said. 'By the time he wakes up, whatever we're doing, it's all over and done with. He's just some dumb poor clown. He helped us one way, and he hurt us another. Listening to him, out there on the water, I kind of felt for him. Okay?'

Parker and Sternberg looked at one another. To be betrayed, to be set up, to be led into an ambush, and then not deal with the guy that did it? On the other hand, it was certainly true that Hanzen wasn't a threat to them any more, and for whatever reason the ambush hadn't worked, and in fact killing was never a good idea unless there were no other ideas.

'And now,' Wycza said, 'he's got a broken

222

jaw, so it's not like he's singin and dancin'.'

Parker shrugged, and so did Sternberg. 'Well, Hanzen was wrong about one thing,' Parker said, as he walked toward the little Hyundai, the car keys in his hand. 'His problems aren't over.'

2

Parker drove. He was probably taking a long way around, going out to the main state road and then north, but he didn't know all the back ways around here, particularly at night. Still, the main point was to get to the cottages before Mike and Noelle did, because they wouldn't know they were riding into an ambush. But they couldn't reach there from the ship until close to three, and even going the long way around Parker could make it by two-thirty.

They were silent most of the way up, but as they neared the dirt road that led in to the cottages Parker said to Sternberg, in the back seat, 'Lou, here's the gun I took off that guard.'

'You've still got your other one? Fine.'

'My idea is,' Parker said, 'Dan and me go in on foot, see what's what. You and the car stay out by the turnoff, watch for Mike and Noelle.'

'Okay. If I hear anything . . .'

'You do what seems best.'

'Right.'

The landmark for the turnoff at night was the Agway, just to the north of it. They kept lights on up there, in the yard and inside the main store building. Everything else for a few miles around was in darkness at this hour, so when they saw those white and red lights, they knew where they were.

There was no traffic at all; they hadn't seen another car in motion in ten minutes. Parker switched down from headlights to running lights as he made the turn, then switched the lights off entirely before he stopped, with the Hyundai maybe four car lengths in from the blacktop, squarely in the middle of the dirt road. All three got out, and Sternberg, holding the guard's gun loosely at his side, said, 'I'll sit against a tree over here.'

Wycza said, 'Let's hope Mike don't take the turn too fast.'

Sternberg said, 'Parker, now he's worried about Hanzen's *car*. You sure this guy is one of us?'

'Promise you won't tell,' Wycza said, and he and Parker walked on down the road.

There was enough moonlight and starlight to make the paler swath of the road stand out from the darker woods all around it. They walked side by side, guns in their hands, Parker near the left edge of the road, Wycza near the right. After a while, their night vision

224

improved, and they could see a little way into the woods on both sides. Except for the quiet crunch of their shoes on the dirt, there was no sound. And though the air was cool, there was no breeze.

Light up ahead. They moved more slowly, and saw the lights still on in their cottage. In the cleared space in front stood the three motorcycles, near Wycza's Lexus and Parker's Subaru. There was no sound, no movement.

Wycza reached across and tapped Parker's arm, then pointed. The lit-up cottage was second from the left. Between the two cottages on the right a pickup truck was parked. It was a convention here.

There was no way to move to the left past the cottages, which is what Parker had wanted to do. But if you went that way you'd be picked up in the lightspill, so he moved to the right instead and followed Wycza around the edge of the clearing to the farthest right-hand cottage and around it into the deeper darkness there.

In that darkness they paused for a whispered discussion. Wyeza said, 'Who's the truck?'

'Wild card.'

'There's somebody somewhere. Down at the landing?'

'If they still think we're coming from there. I'll look.'

'I'll see what's in the cottage.'

225

'Fine,' Parker said, and went first, around the riverside end of the first cottage and straight out to the drop-off, then left to the wooden stairs down to the river, which were just beyond the range of illumination from the house.

The sound here was river against shore, river against support posts; faint whispers of wavelets, not much louder than Parker and Wycza had been, a minute ago.

Parker went silently down the uneven steps. There was no comfortable place for somebody to sit and wait on the steep slope to either side, and there was nobody on the dock. The river reflected moonlight and made a heavy steady sweeping movement from right to left.

Parker went back up the stairs, and at the top he stood and waited and listened. At first he heard and saw nothing, but then he caught the movement as the outside door to the screened porch of their cottage pushed inward, the screen of the door reflecting light differently as it moved. He looked lower, and could just make out Wycza crawling through the doorway, flat on his belly. The screen door eased shut.

Parker moved to his left, to get to the rear of the last cottage, where they'd split up, so he could follow Wycza's route. He turned at that cottage, moved along its screened-in porch, and beyond it saw to his left the pickup, parked facing this way, as though the driver

226

hadn't considered the possibility he might want to leave in a hurry.

As Parker crossed the open space to the next cottage, there were two sudden shots. He dove to the ground, pressed against the stone foundation of the cottage, and lay prone, Python held in both hands on the ground in front of him.

The shots had come from out ahead, probably their cottage. And the two shots had been different, the first one lighter, more of a clap, the second one heavier, a full-throated bark. The kind of sound this Python might make, or Wycza's 27.

Parker waited for some sort of follow-up, but nothing else happened, so he snaked forward along the ground, pulling himself on with his elbows, arms crossed in front of his jaw, Python pointed at the screened porch beside him.

At the corner, he was where the light began. He looked across at the yellow windows, and waited. After a minute, he heard movement, walking; somebody who wasn't trying to conceal himself. Then the front door opened and slammed shut, and a few seconds later Wycza appeared around the corner down there, 27 in his hand but casually pointed downward. He looked this way and that, but not warily, along the ground, like somebody who's lost a cufflink. He stopped to look at the window to the bedroom off the kitchen,

227

fingering the screen there. Then he came on, and Parker could hear he was singing, not loud, not soft: 'Be down to getcha in a taxi, honey, better be ready 'bout half past eight.'

Wycza was not somebody who sang. As he rounded the corner and walked openly past the doorway he'd crawled through just a couple of minutes ago, Parker reversed himself and got crouching to his feet, and hurried bent low back the way he'd come, to the last cottage, and around it to the front, where he saw Wycza just moving out of the range of the light toward the road. He didn't seem to care that he was exposed.

Keeping to the darkness, being sure he couldn't be seen, Parker followed.

3

Down the dirt road, where you couldn't see the light from the cottage any more, Wycza stood waiting. Parker joined him and said, 'What's up?'

'The three bikers, like you said, in three rooms. Set up for an ambush, but gunned down. Two dead, one not. Not then.'

'Wounded? Took a shot at you.'

'The young one. Been hit high on the chest, right side, lying in the living room behind the sofa. Looked dead. I found the other two first, one in a bedroom, shot in the back of the head, one in the kitchen, shot in the chest. One shot each.'

'Economical.'

'I was keepin' down, movin' slow.' Wycza shook his head, remembering. 'All of a sudden, this son of a bitch in the living room rolls over, he's got a .22 in his hand. You know as well as I do, you can't hit your own pocket with one of those.'

'They're not for work,' Parker agreed. 'For noise, and for show.'

'So he shot at me, hit the ceiling or some fucking thing, and I put him down.'

'Okay.'

'The thing is,' Wycza said, 'he startled me, so I come upright, and I did him, and I'm standin' there, and all at once I realize, I got windows on three sides of me. You know that living room, it's all across the front.'

'But nobody killed you,' Parker said.

'Hell of a way to find out,' Wycza said. 'So where's the guy from the pickup? Those three in the cottage didn't shoot each other, and the pickup's still there, but nobody's shooting at me. Is he hurt? Or is he just waiting? Did somebody maybe put a bullet into the pickup guy?'

'Not with a .22,' Parker said.

'The one in the kitchen,' Wycza said, 'carried a .45 auto, been fired once tonight.'

'That's different,' Parker said.

229

'So I figure,' Wycza said, 'long as nobody's shooting at me anyway, why not just waltz around, have a look?'

'I watched you,' Parker told him.

'You weren't the only one, I'm pretty sure,' Wycza said. 'So you saw me stop at the bedroom window.'

'You were interested in that screen.'

'Three fresh holes in it, two pushing in, one pushing out. The way it looks to me,' Wycza said, 'those three were scattered in the house for the ambush. Our pickup guy came over, shot the one in the bedroom. The other one ran over through the kitchen, got to the doorway, saw the pickup guy in the window, took a shot at him, the pickup guy shot him back. Or the other way around. Anyway, the biker dead, the pickup guy wounded. Some blood drops on the wall, like it sprayed when he was hit.'

'But he went on after the third one.'

'Well, he had to,' Wycza said. 'In a hurry, hurt, got him in the living room through the side window there, another hole in the screen. But he didn't feel healthy enough to go in and finish the job. Went to hide, hope to feel better, wait for us. But from what I could see, it's only the one guy.'

Parker turned and looked back toward the cottages. 'So he's there, probably in the cottage between ours and his truck—'

'That's where I'd put him,' Wycza agreed.

'Where he can watch, but where he can also feel like he's got a way out if he needs it.'

'And he's wounded, or maybe he's dead now,' Parker said. 'Wounded bad, or just scraped.'

'He didn't take a shot at me,' Wycza pointed out.

'Waiting for the money,' Parker said. 'If he's alive, that's what he's doing.'

Wycza nodded. 'That's what I'd do, I was him. And alive.'

'If we burn him out,' Parker said, 'the flames'll bring every volunteer fireman in a hundred miles. If we just go in to get him, he's got too many chances to get us first.'

'Fuck him, leave him there,' Wycza said.

'I can't do that,' Parker said. 'Come on, let's go talk to Lou.'

4

Before they reached the main road, they saw headlights turn in, then go black. 'The money's here,' Wycza said.

They continued on, and found the van stopped behind the Hyundai, its sliding side door open, spilling light onto the road. Mike Carlow, without his chauffeur's cap and coat, stood beside the van listening to Lou Sternberg explain the situation, while Noelle

231

sat in the van doorway, feet flat on the ground as she leaned against the side wall to her right. She was still in her invalid filmy white, and she looked like a ghost.

'Here they are now,' Sternberg said.

Wycza said, 'Noelle? You okay?'

'Not yet,' she told him, 'but I will be.'

'She got dried out,' Carlow explained. 'What's the situation back there?'

'Three dead bikers,' Parker said. 'The one that got them's holed up in another cabin, waiting for the money. He's wounded, we don't know how bad.'

Sternberg said, 'They fought each other even before they got the goods?'

'No, it's somebody else. No idea who.'

Carlow said, 'He gunned down three bikers by himself, and now he's in there waiting to take us down?'

Wycza said, 'He's ambitious, we know that much.'

Sternberg said, 'We're here, the money's here. Let him stay and rot, we'll go somewhere else.'

Parker said, 'I need to know who he is.'

'*I* don't,' Sternberg said.

Parker said, 'But who is this guy? Where'd he come from? Is he going to be behind me some day?'

'He won't be behind *me*,' Sternberg said. 'I'll be home in London.'

'What I'm thinking about,' Parker said, 'is

Cathman. I've been waiting for something from him, and I'm wondering is this it.'

Wycza said, 'Cathman? Parker, from the way you describe that guy Cathman, that isn't him back there.'

'No, but he could be *from* him.'

'Parker,' Sternberg said, 'you understand the situation. You've got a link with this Cathman, the rest of us don't. He may know your name and your phone number, but he doesn't know a damn thing about me. You got a guy laying in ambush down in there? Fine, let him lay, I'm going home. We did good work tonight, and I'm ready to see the money, put it in my pocket, call British Air in the morning.'

'I've got to go along with Lou,' Noelle said. 'I'm tired, and I feel like shit, and all I want to do is sleep and eat and drink. I don't want to fight anymore.'

'Okay, you're right,' Parker said. 'Whoever this guy is, he's my problem, not any of yours. Mike, can you get the van around this car or do I need to move it out of the way?'

Carlow said, 'You need to move it, if I'm going in. Why am I going in?'

'Just to get away from the road, so no county cop comes along while we're splitting the take.'

Carlow laughed and said, '*That* would be a moment. Yeah, move it over. Noelle, honey, you wanna get in or you wanna get out?'

For answer, she hunkered back and drew

her legs up under her. Seated in the van doorway, crosslegged, slumped forward, she looked like an untrustworthy oracle.

Parker jigged the Hyundai forward and back to the side of the road, waited while Carlow drove around him, then got out and walked with the others after the van. They were all stained red when the brake lights came on, and then it was dark again, except for the van's interior light, gleaming on the ghostly Noelle.

Carlow climbed from the driver's seat into the back of the van and slid the box out from the wheelchair. It was crammed full of the white plastic bags, four of them.

'Excuse me, Noelle,' Sternberg said, and climbed up past her into the van. The rear seats had been removed in there, to make room for the wheelchair, which was now pushed as far back as possible, leaving a gray-carpeted open area. Carlow and Sternberg and Noelle sat on the carpet in this area, facing in, and began to count the money, while Parker and Wycza stood outside, sometimes watching, sometimes looking and listening up and down the road.

Three hundred nineteen thousand, seven hundred twenty dollars. Parker had had three thousand in expenses, that he took out first. Sternberg did the math on the rest, and said, 'That's sixty-three thousand, three hundred forty four apiece.'

'You each take sixty-three,' Parker said. 'I'll

take the change for dealing with the guy back there.'

'A bargain,' Carlow said.

Noelle had a handbag that would carry her share, and the others used the white plastic bags. In Parker's bag, there was sixty-seven thousand, seven hundred twenty dollars.

The four of them would take the van, leaving the Hyundai, which nobody wanted. Wycza said, 'Coming out, use the Lexus. The key's in the ashtray.'

'I will,' Parker agreed. 'Lou, I'll take back that other gun now.'

'Right.' Sternberg handed it to him, and said, 'Call me again sometime.'

'I will.'

Carlow drove, Wycza in the seat beside him, Sternberg and Noelle seated on the floor in back. Only the back-up lights were on as Carlow backed past the Hyundai and out to the main road. Parker stood watching, and saw the van's headlights come on as it swung out and away, to the right.

Darkness again. It would take a few minutes to get his night vision back. He had the Python in his left hip pocket, and held the automatic in his right hand, the bag of money in his left. He walked down the road toward the cottages, and when he could see a little better he chose a spot where there was a thick double-trunked maple just to the right of the road. He went around behind it, put the plastic bag on the ground against its trunk, and brushed some dirt and stones and decayed leaves over it.

As he straightened, headlights came, fast, from the cottages. He stayed behind the tree, and the pickup went by, racing too hard for this road, jouncing all over the place. Whoever was at the wheel was impossible to see, and more than impossible to shoot.

The pickup lunged by. Parker stepped out into the roadway and listened, and there was a sudden shriek of brakes when the driver came across the Hyundai.

No crash, though; he managed to get around it. Then silence.

Parker put the Python in his right hand, and walked on toward the cottages.

5

Now there were lights in two cottages, including the one where Parker and Wycza had decided the unknown shooter must be holed up. Parker was certain there was nobody left alive back here, but he was cautious anyway. He took the same route as last time, around to the right, beyond the reach of the glowing windows. Around the last cottage, then hunkered low to go past the space between cottages, where the pickup used to be parked. And then, silently but swiftly, across

236

the screened-in porch to the cottage that was now lit up.

When Parker had checked out all the cottages, back when they'd first moved in here, this back door had not been locked, and it still wasn't. He stepped through into the kitchen, and it was dark, the lit rooms farther away, living room and bath.

Parker listened. Nothing. He crossed the kitchen to the hall doorway, and stopped. Nothing. He went into the hall and looked through the bathroom doorway at a mess. Half a roll of paper towels on the sink, bloody individual paper towels in the sink and the bathtub and on the floor. Blood smears on the sink.

The dark bedrooms he passed were empty, and showed no signs of use. In the living room, a floor lamp at one end of the sofa was lit, shining down on a dark stain on the flower-pattern slipcover. Parker crossed to look at the stain, and it was blood, some dry, some still sticky. It made an irregular pattern, just at the end of the sofa.

Wounded. Wycza had been right about that, about the blood spatters on the outside wall next door. Head-shot, it looked like, except the guy was too active for that. He'd managed, after he'd been shot, to go on and kill the third biker.

But he hadn't had the strength to switch the lights off. He had to know Parker and the

237

others had gone away with the place dark, and would know something was wrong if they came back and it was all lit up. But he hadn't had the strength to do anything about it. He'd come over here to collapse, to try to get his strength back.

So it wasn't that he'd let Wycza live, in order to wait for the rest to show up with the money. He had passed out over here, he'd never seen Wycza at all.

And then came to. Patched himself one way and another, and took off, knowing the ambush was ruined, the money wouldn't be coming here.

Where would he go now? Who the hell was he?

Maybe Cathman had some answers.

6

It was a long night, and getting longer. Parker had walked out the dirt road to get the plastic bag of money and bring it back here and now it was inside the window well of the right rear door of the Lexus. The automatic he'd taken from the guard on the ship had been flung out over the slope into the river. The two simple incendiaries had been set, one in each lit cottage. There would be no surfaces for the technicians to scan for fingerprints. There'd be

238

plenty left here, though, to give the law things to think about.

If he'd done the fuses right, the two fires should start three hours from now, after seven in the morning; daylight, so they could burn longer before being noticed. Yawning, forcing himself to stay awake, Parker got behind the wheel of the Lexus and steered it out to the main road, intending to head north, to deal with Cathman, one way or another. But when he saw the Hyundai, he stopped.

He rubbed his eyes, and the grizzle on his face. Wycza had been wrong, dammit. He had the big man's flaw of every once in a while feeling sorry for the weak.

Greg Hanzen knew their faces, he knew a link to Parker through Pete Rudd, he could describe the getaway from the ship. He could let the law know for sure that the money had not come off with the heisters. And his car was here, next to a scene of a lot of trouble that had to be connected with the robbery, and no way for Parker to get rid of it.

Cathman was to the north, Albany, an hour away. Hanzen was half an hour to the south, at his landing. Or, if he was conscious by now, maybe he'd made his way to a hospital somewhere, a river rat with a broken jaw on a night when a major robbery takes place on the river. Would the cops ask him questions?

I've got to look, Parker told himself. If he's there, that's that. If he's gone, I don't pursue it, I let it play out as it plays.

He turned right and drove south. Ten minutes later, he saw the first lights he'd seen, a 24-hour gas station and convenience store. He filled the tank and bought a coffee and a glazed sugar doughnut, and drove on south, finishing the coffee just before the turnoff in to Hanzen's landing.

He switched off his headlights as he crossed the railroad tracks, and ahead he saw the glow of some other light. He stopped in the clearing, got out of the Lexus, and the light came from Hanzen's boat, still beached up on to the shore. A not-very-bright light was on in the cabin, and the cabin door was open, facing the river.

Parker didn't get into the boat; he was too tired to climb over the side. He held the Python in his right hand and walked down beside the boat until the water was ankle-deep, cold inside his shoes, where he could look back in at the cabin, and Hanzen was in there. He was awake and miserable, hunched over his battery lantern. He'd tied a towel under his jaw and over the top of his head, like somebody in a comic strip with a toothache. He sensed Parker, and looked at him with watery eyes. 'Now what?' he said. His speech was mushy.

Parker said, 'I came to tell you, your problems are over after all.'

7

Driving north toward Albany on the Taconic Parkway, Parker watched both dawn and a heavy cloud cover move in from the west. He drove with the windows open, for the rush of air to keep him awake.

One more detail, and it was over. He'd take a motel room, sleep the day and night away, not try to get back to Claire until tomorrow.

Howell should never have given Cathman Parker's name and phone number. When he'd done it, of course, Howell hadn't known he'd soon be dead, unable to keep control of what was going on. Still, he shouldn't have exposed Parker this way.

Before Claire, it was simpler. Then, there was no phone number that would reach Parker, no 'address' where you could put your hand and touch him. It was harder now to stay remote, but it could still be done. It was just more work, that's all.

North, and then west, over the Hudson toward Albany and the gray day. It was after six, and there was starting to be traffic, early-morning workers. Once Parker left highway to drive on city streets, there were a few school buses.

Delmar was still mostly asleep. The supermarket where he'd left the Subaru when he'd visited Cathman at home that one time was not yet open, and the blacktop expanse of its parking lot was empty. One of the few houses in the neighborhood with lights gleaming inside the windows was Cathman's, both upstairs and down. And in the next block, parked on the right side of the street in front of a two-family house, was the pickup truck.

Parker drove on another half block, looking at the pickup in his rearview mirror, and there was no question. He stopped the Lexus, rolled up its windows, locked it, and walked back to the pickup.

It had some new dents and scratches on it. There was a rental company decal just under the right headlight, like a teardrop. The guy had gone away without locking the truck, and when Parker opened the driver's door to look inside there was a little dried blood on the seatback; not a lot, but some.

These trucks have storage spaces behind the bench seats. Parker tilted the seatback forward, and looked at a shotgun. It too had a decal on it, like the truck, this one smaller, gold letters on black, on the side of the butt, just above the base. It read 'MONROVILLE P.D.'

Monroville? Did he know that name? And what was this guy doing with a police department shotgun?

And how come he was visiting Cathman?

Parker didn't feel tired any more. He

242

shut the pickup's door, and walked toward Cathman's house, number 437.

8

As before, shades were drawn over the windows of the enclosed porch downstairs and the front windows above. Light gleamed behind the shades, upstairs and down.

Parker took the same route in as when he'd come here wearing the utility company jacket. This time, it was early morning, nobody around, no traffic on this residential side street, so he just walked forward as though he belonged here. With the shades drawn in the house, nobody could watch the outside without shifting a shade, making a movement that he would see.

The kitchen door was locked again, and the lock still didn't matter. He went through it, and then stopped to listen. Nothing; no sound anywhere.

Slowly he moved through the house. Three lamps burned in the living room, but no one was there. Two magazines and a newspaper lay messily beside one armchair.

Parker continued on, checked the enclosed porch, and the entire downstairs was empty. The staircase leading up was dark, but light shone around the corner up there. He held the

Python across his chest and went up sideways, slowly. The stairs were carpeted, and though the carpet was worn the steps didn't squeak.

There was a short upstairs hall, with doorways off it, none of the doors closed. Two of the rooms showed light, and from his last time here he knew the one on the left was Cathman's bedroom, and the one at the end was his office.

The dark room on the right was empty, and so was its closet. Cathman himself was in his bedroom, in bed, asleep, curled up on his side, frowning. The ceiling light and a bedside lamp were both lit. Parker silently crossed the room and checked the closet, and no one was hiding there.

No one else was upstairs at all. Parker came last to the office, and it was empty, too, and where the hell was the guy from the pickup truck? It made sense he was linked to Cathman some way, that had made sense from the time he showed up at the cottages, and it made even more sense when his pickup was parked a block from here. But Cathman is sleeping with his lights on, and there's nobody else around, so something in the equation doesn't make sense after all.

The last time Parker had been in this house the office had been the neatest room in it, as though Cathman were demonstrating his professionalism to himself, convincing himself he deserved a hearing and respect and a job. This time, three or four sheets of lined paper were askew on the desk, covered with handwriting in black ink, with a lot of editing and second thoughts.

What's with Cathman now? Why was he afraid to sleep in the dark? What idea is he trying so hard to express?

Standing over the desk, Python in right hand, Parker moved the sheets around with his left index finger. The writing was very neat and legible, a bureaucrat's penmanship, but there were a lot of crossings-out and inserted additions. Numbers in circles were at the top left of each page. Parker picked up the page marked '1' and read:

'Gambling is not only a vice itself, but is an attraction to other vice. Theft, prostitution, usury, drug dealing and more, all follow in gambling's train.'

Oh; it was his dead horse again, still being beaten. Parker was about to put the page back down on the desk, but something tugged at his attention, and he skimmed the page to the bottom, then went on to page 2, and began to see that this was more than just the dead horse, more than just Cathman's usual whine. This time, he was building toward something, some point, some deal . . .

'Knowing the dangers, seeing those dangers ignored by the elected officials around me, believing it was my duty to expose the dangers and give the people of the State of New York the opportunity to choose for themselves what path they might take, I have, for some time, cultivated contacts with certain underworld characters. I felt very out of place among these people, but I knew it was my duty to stay with them. I was convinced that the presence of so much cash money on that gambling ship, so large and obvious and available, would have to attract criminals, as bees are attracted to the honey pot. And now we see I was right.'

This was it, this was coming to the point at last. There'd always been something wrong about Cathman, something that didn't ring true, and it was tied up with his fixation on gambling. And now Parker himself had made an appearance in this diatribe, along with Marshall Howell, and the others, all of them certain underworld characters. And all to what purpose?

Parker read on. More pounding on the dead horse, more self-congratulation. Parker skimmed to the bottom, and moved on to page 3, and midway down it he read:

'My recent contacts with career criminals have made it possible for me to be of very material assistance in capturing the gang involved in the crime and also in recovering at least part of the stolen money. In return for my assistance, which could be obtained nowhere else, and which I am offering freely and completely, I would expect proper publicity for my contribution to the solution of this crime.

246

That publicity must include my reasons for having sought out these criminals in the first place, which is my conviction that gambling inevitably brings crime in its wake. I would need the opportunity to make these views widely known to the public. I would insist on at least one press conference . . .'

Insane. The son of a bitch is insane. The dead horse is riding *him*. He's so determined to prove that gambling leads to crime that he's got to rig the crime. He went out to find people to commit the crime for him; first Howell, then Parker. Point them at the ship, give them every bit of help they want, so after they do their job he can say, 'See? I was right. Gambling led to the robbery, so shut down the gambling ship. And listen to me from now on, don't shunt me off into retirement, as though I was old and useless and not valuable any more.'

There was no way to make that fly. Was he so far gone into his own dreams, his own fantasy, that he didn't see it couldn't work?

Does Cathman really believe he can tell the law he knows details about a robbery, but he won't give them over unless he gets a press conference? If he clams up, that's already a crime. He'll have no choice, once he sends this goddam manifesto to whoever he's going to send it to—the governor, probably being the megalomaniac lunatic he is—he'll have no choice but to tell the law everything he knows.

247

And everything he knows is Parker.

'—at the tone seven-thirty. Expect high clouds today, seasonable temperatures ...'

Cathman's radio alarm clock. It went on, talking about this and that, and soon it would tell Cathman his designer robbery had come off according to plan. Time he should type up that letter neat and send it out.

Along with what? What else would Cathman have to give? Parker's name and phone number written down somewhere. Maybe a diary? How much of his own involvement with the heist was he figuring to admit? (They'd get the whole thing out of him in five minutes, which he wouldn't be likely to realize.)

Cathman is a danger and an irritation and a lunatic, but he has to be talked to, for just a little while, to make sure all of the danger and all of the lunacy is known about. What else are Cathman and his idle hands up to?

Parker folded the four pages, folded them again, put them in his left hip pocket. Then he picked up the Python from the desk and walked down the hall and stopped in the bedroom doorway.

Cathman lay on his back now, pajama'd arms over the covers, still frowning as he stared at the ceiling. He didn't notice Parker right away, and when the excited news announcer began the story of last night's robbery all he did was close his eyes, as though the effort to make that robbery happen had merely left him exhausted.

'Turn it off,' Parker said.

Cathman's eyes snapped open. He stared at Parker in terror. He didn't move.

Parker pointed the Python at the radio. 'Turn it off or I shoot it off.'

Cathman blinked at the gun, at Parker's face, at the radio. At last he hunched himself up onto his left elbow and reached over to shut it off. Then he moved upward in the bed so he could slump with his back against the headboard. He looked dull, weary, as though his sleep had not been restful. He said, 'I didn't know you'd come here. I didn't think you'd actually give me the money.'

Parker almost laughed at him. 'Give you the money? I just read your confession.'

'My con—? Oh. That's not a confession.'

'The cops will think it is.'

Cathman sat up straighter, smoothing the covers with his hands, looking at Parker more carefully. He had finally realized his survival was at issue here. He said, 'You don't think I intend to mail that, do you?'

'With copies to the media.'

'Certainly not,' Cathman said. He was a bureaucrat, he lied effortlessly. He said, 'It occurred to me, there was a remote possibility you people might get caught, and then, what if you implicated me? In that case, I had that letter to show, the letter I would have said I

249

was just about to mail.'

'What else—' Parker said, and too late he saw Cathman's eyes shift, and something solid shut down his brain.

9

Voices, far away, down a yellow tunnel, then rushing forward:

'All I want is the money.'

'Why would I know where any—'

'You ran this thing! It's *your* rob—!'

'I never did! I'm not a thief!'

'He's *here*. Look, look at him, he's here.'

Handcuffs, behind back. Pain, in small mean lightning bolts, in the back of the head.

'I didn't know he was coming here, I never thought he—'

'I've been watching. You think you can lie to me, I've watched this house. He was here before, dressed like from the electric company, he spent *hours* here—'

'I never *expected* him to—'

'I'm thinking, who is this guy? He's not from the electric company, breaking in, staying hours.'

'He wasn't supposed to—'

'You came home. You talked with him.'

'He was in my—'

'You drank *wine* with him!'

Lying on the floor. Legs free, That idiot Cathman silent now. This one isn't connected to Cathman after all, he was following him, watching him. Why?

'I didn't hear everything you said, I came over after you came home, I listened at the side window. You called him Parker and he said he needed police ID and there was something about an assemblyman and you asked him when he was going to commit the robbery and he wouldn't tell you.'

This one has been here all along, bird-dogging, waiting for it to happen. Who the hell is he? Where did he come from?

Cathman finally had his voice back: 'You've still got it wrong. I'm afraid of that gun of yours, I won't pretend I'm not, but you're still wrong. I don't know where the money is. You'll have to ask *him*, if you didn't kill him.'

'I didn't kill him, but let's wake him up. Go get a glass of water from the bathroom.'

'I'm awake.'

Parker rolled over on to his back, as much as he could with his hands cuffed behind him, and tried not to wince. When he moved, the pain in his head gave an extra little kick. He opened his eyes and squinted upward.

The guy was youngish, pudgy, thick-necked, in wrinkled chinos and a pale blue dress shirt; Parker had never seen him before in his life. His right ear was covered by a bulky makeshift bandage, what looked like a length of duct tape over several thicknesses of toilet paper. A red scar pointed to the bandage along his right cheekbone.

The biker back at the cottages had come very close, almost close enough. The .45 automatic slug does a lot of damage even on the near misses, and that's what this had been. The bullet scraped facial bone, took out an ear, and kept going.

Parker nodded at the bandage. 'You got any ear left down in there?'

The guy looked surprised, and almost glad 'Are you wising off with *me*?'

'Tell him, Mr Parker,' Cathman said. 'Tell him I have nothing to do with it.'

The guy laughed. He enjoyed being in charge. 'Oh, now he's *mister*, is he?' He held a little .38 revolver in his right hand, which he pointed at Parker as he said, 'I bet, if I shoot you in the ankle, and then ask a question, you'll answer it. Whadaya think?'

'I think this is the wrong neighborhood for gunshots,' Parker said. 'I think it'll fill up with cops, and I don't think anybody in this room wants that. If you'd like to think with your brain instead of your gun, reach in my left hip pocket and read Cathman's confession.'

That threw the guy off-stride. 'His what?'

Cathman babbled, 'It was a letter, I was never going to send it, I needed a—'

'Read it,' Parker said. With difficulty, he rolled the other way. 'Then we can talk.'

252

The guy was cautious, and not completely an amateur. He came the long way around Parker, staying away from his feet, crouching down behind him, touched the barrel of the revolver to the back of his neck, and held it there while he pulled the folded pages out of his pocket. Then he stood and backed away to the doorway, where Parker could see him again.

Cathman said, 'I have to go to the bathroom.'

The guy was struggling to unfold the pages while not letting go of the gun or looking away from Parker. Distracted, he said, 'Go on, go on.'

Cathman, looking like a large sad child in his yellow and green striped pajamas, got out of the bed and padded barefoot into the connecting bathroom, while the guy got the pages open at last and started to read.

Parker rolled again and managed to sit up, then moved backward until he could lean against the foot of the bed. He looked around on the floor and didn't see the Python, so it was probably in the guy's pocket. He watched him read, and thought about how to deal with this situation.

'Jesus Christ.' The guy had finished. He dropped the pages on the floor and looked at Parker and said, 'He's a fucking lunatic.'

'Yes, he is.'

'He set you up to do it, so he could turn you

in. That isn't even entrapment, I don't knew what the fuck that is.'

'Stupidity.'

'All right.' The guy was more relaxed now, as though Cathman being an amateur and an idiot had created a bond between the two of them. He said, 'So if you didn't come here to divvy up the money, or anything like that, why did you come?'

'To kill him.'

'Hah. No loose ends.'

'That's right.'

'I wish I'd done it that way myself, years ago,' the guy said. 'All right, Mr Parker, I want in. I've got you, but I don't want you, I want money. Are your partners dead, too?'

'No. We know each other, we work together.'

'So they're waiting for you to come back, mission accomplished, the loose cannon dealt with.'

'Right. And we divvy the money and go our ways.'

'So if I kill you,' the guy said, 'I can't find them, and I can't get any money. But if I let you live, I've got to have money. I need money, that's what it comes down to.'

'I could see that.'

'So what's your offer?'

'We got over four hundred thousand,' Parker said.

The guy frowned. 'The radio said three and

254

a half.'

'I don't know about that. Usually they estimate high. All I know is, we got over four.' Because, to make his story work, there had to seem to be enough for everybody. 'There's five of us, so that's eighty apiece, a little more than eighty. You help me in two ways, and—'

'Like letting you live.'

Parker shook his head. 'You aren't gonna kill me, because I'm not a threat to you like this, and I'm no use to you dead. Don't talk as though we're both ignorant.'

'Well, fuck me,' the guy said, with a surprised laugh. 'You talk pretty tough for somebody sitting under my gun. You think I never killed anybody?'

'I think you never killed anybody when you didn't have a reason for it,' Parker said. 'Do you want to listen to my proposition?'

The guy shrugged. 'Help you two ways, you said.'

'First, kill Cathman. I need him dead. I can't do it myself laced up like this, so either you do it or unhook me so I can do it myself.'

'We'll work on that,' the guy said. 'What's the other?'

'For that, I do need to be unhooked,' Parker said.

'I don't think so. For what?'

'I've got to search in here and in the office. I've got to see what else he put on paper that could make trouble for me.'

'I'll search for you. You tell me what you're looking for.'

'No.'

The guy looked at him, and waited, and then said, 'No? That's it, no?'

'That's it. No. Do you want to hear what your side is?'

'This should be good.'

'Why not? If you kill Cathman, or let me do it, and let me run my search in here, that makes you a partner. I won't have trouble with the others, so neither will you. We'll each be getting a little over eighty. So we take twelve out of each of us, that still gives us almost seventy apiece, which is still good, and sixty for you. Is sixty enough for you?'

Clearly, the guy would try to figure out how to get it all, how not to have any partners at the end of the day, but just as clearly he'd also try to figure out how to make it look as though he was content with a piece. Should he pretend to think sixty was enough? Parker watched him think it through, and at last the guy grinned a little and said, 'If things'd worked out the way I wanted, I'd have it all. Tell me why didn't you come back to the cabins.'

'You were there?' Parker said. 'Did you by any chance run into some bikers?'

The guy's hand moved toward his wounded ear, but then lowered again. He said, 'You know about them.'

'We had a guy with a boat,' Parker told him,

256

'for when we left the ship. He sold us out to those people, but when we got in his boat it didn't feel right, so we made him tell us what he'd done.'

'So where did you go instead?'

'His landing. He's got a place upstream from the cottages, we went there. He had a whole operation up there, a shack by the water, he grows marijuana in peat moss bags suspended on the water. That's his link with the bikers, he's the farmer, they're the processors.'

'A shack on the water,' the guy said. 'I've heard about that peat moss business, it's been tried before. Is that where your partners are, the shack?'

'Yes.'

'Telephone there?'

'Of course not.'

'And where's the boat guy?'

'In the river.'

The guy thought it over. Parker let him have a minute, but then figured it was time to distract him: 'Cathman's been gone quite a while.'

'What?' Startled, the guy called, 'Cathman!' When there was no answer, he strode over to the shut door and hit it twice with the gun butt. Then he pulled open the door and took one step in, and stopped.

Parker said, 'Pills?'

The guy stepped back from the doorway.

'Well, there's one from your wish list. Or almost. The color of his face, the sounds in his throat, if we called nine one one right now and got the EMT over here on the double, they just might save him. What do you think?'

'I think,' Parker said, 'we should respect his wishes.'

10

Parker thought he was probably a cop. The way he handled I himself, some of the things he'd said, turns of phrase. And the shotgun in the truck being from a police department. And that he just happened to be traveling with handcuffs.

Some kind of rogue cop, running away from trouble he'd made for himself, needing a bankroll to start over. Somehow, he'd heard about the ship heist, decided to deal himself in. Wound up at the cottages, same as the three bikers, so all they did was screw up each other's ambush.

The question was, where was his road in? It seemed as though it had to be one of the other four people in the job, but none of them looked right for the part. It hadn't been Cathman, who'd had a different agenda, it wasn't Parker, so who else could it be?

Dan Wycza; Lou Sternberg; Mike Carlow;

Noelle Braselle. He couldn't see this mangled cop cozying up with any of them.

Anyway, if it was one of them, wouldn't this guy know more than he does? But what else could it be?

Maybe, a little later, he'd get a chance to ask that question. But for now, they still had to negotiate their way through this matter of the search. Parker needed to make that search, because the alternative was to uproot Claire and start all over again somewhere else, and if he did that this time he'd be doing it again, and Claire wouldn't be happy on the constant go. Claire liked a nest.

'In here,' Parker said, meaning in the bedroom, 'you can do it for me. Open drawers, take out anything that's paper, throw it on the bed, let me look at it, and we take away what I want. In the office down the hall there, we could do it this way. I go first, and stop in the doorway. You undo the cuffs, and I walk forward to the desk, so you're always behind me. You stay in the doorway with the gun on me. I do my search. Then I walk backward to the door with my wrists behind my back, you cuff me again. Or you could just cuff me in front, then I could—'

The guy laughed at him. 'Sure,' he said. 'Cuff you in front. I could ask you to hold my gun for me, too.'

'Then the other way. You're behind me, you're armed, if I try to do something you

259

don't have to kill me, just wound me. What am I gonna do about you at the desk? Throw a pen at you?'

'I'll have to search it first,' the guy said. 'Maybe you happen to know there's a gun in one of those drawers.'

'Cathman, with a gun? Search away. You want to help me to my feet?'

'No,' the guy said, and backed into the hall. 'I don't need to be that close to you, you'll work it out.'

Of course he would. Well, it had been worth a try. Using the foot of the bed to push against, Parker turned himself partway around, got one leg under his torso, and pushed upward against the bed until he was on one knee. From there it was easier, except for one second when he wasn't sure he'd keep his balance. But he did, again by leaning on the bed, and there he was, standing.

'I knew you could do it,' the guy said. 'Come on out, lead the way. We'll do this office first.'

They went down the hall and into the office, and the guy had Parker stand in the corner between the two windowed walls, facing the wall, while he did a quick open-slam of all the drawers in the desk. Then he said, 'Okay, good. A lotta shit in here, you ask me. Back up to the door.'

Parker did, and felt the vibrations of metal scraping on metal as the key moved around the lock.

'Stand still, I'm doing this one-handed.'

'Right.'

The cuffs came off. 'Walk.'

Parker walked. His head still ached, and now his wrists were sore. He rubbed them as he walked across the room, giving himself a fireman's grip and kneading the wrists, and then sat at the desk.

A lot of shit in the drawers, as the guy had said, but not all of it useless. He palmed a paper clip, one of the larger thicker ones, and when he bent to open the bottom drawer he clipped it to the front of his shirt, below desk level. There were also ballpoint pens, simple plain ones that didn't retract. He held one up, showing it to the guy in the doorway, saying, 'I could use a pen. Okay?'

The guy snickered at him. 'To throw at me?'

'Sure.'

'You want it, keep it.'

Parker dropped the pen in his shirt pocket, and kept searching, and at the end he had two pages from this year's weekly memo book, one with Marshall Howell's name and his own written there (the name 'Parker' was followed by a question mark), and one with that phone number of his that Howell had given away. He had also smeared his palms over everything he'd touched. There was nothing else here either of danger or of use.

He held up the two torn-off pieces of paper and said, 'I want to pocket these.'

261

The guy shrugged. His carelessness meant it didn't matter what Parker did to avoid the law, he was dead meat anyway. He said, 'Go ahead, you aren't armed.'

Heisters don't say *armed*, they say *carrying* or *heavy*, because a gun will be heavy in the pocket. Cops are armed. They don't carry their guns in a pocket.

'I'm done,' Parker said, the two papers stowed away.

'Show me your hands.'

'Sure.' Parker held up empty hands, turned them to show the palms and the backs, fingers splayed out.

'Okay. Now do like we said. Stand up, turn around, back over to me.'

Parker stood, and as he turned he slid the paperclip into his right hand, held between the ball of the palm and the side of the thumb. The fingers of both hands were curled slightly. He backed across the room, seeing the guy indistinctly in the window ahead of him and to the right, and the guy backed across the hall. Very careful, very anxious.

'Okay, stop there.'

Parker stopped. The cold metal closed on his wrists again, and he heard the double snap. The guy tugged once on the cuffs to be sure they were locked in place, then said, 'Okay, let's go.'

'The bedroom.'

'Fine, fine.'

Parker went first, and in the bedroom he said, 'I need those papers you dropped on the floor. Don't tell me to pick them up, all right?'

The guy laughed. 'I'll help you out,' he said. 'Go stand on the other side of the bed.' Too far away to kick him in the face, in other words.

'Sure,' Parker said, and walked over there, and through the open bathroom doorway he could see the mound of yellow and green striped cloth huddled between sink and toilet, like the laundry waiting for the maid. Well, you made a lot of trouble, Cathman, Parker thought, but tomorrow people will still pay money to see the next card.

The guy picked up Cathman's four-page fantasy and put it in his own left side trouser pocket. He said, 'Anything else?'

'Drawers. Dresser, bedside table. Anything paper.'

'I know, I know, toss it on the bed. You stay over there.'

'Naturally.'

While the guy was opening and closing drawers, Parker carefully shifted the paperclip to a more secure position, inside his curled fingers. The search was indifferent, but complete, and produced very little paper. Theater tickets, a medical prescription, a crossword puzzle magazine. Parker looked at it all, scattered on the bed, and thought at least some of this stuff would give this guy's fingerprints to the law; the shiny magazine cover, for instance. He had to know it himself, so he had to already be in too deep shit to worry about such things. Which meant he wasn't exactly careless—in fact, he was very careful—but he was reckless. So he'd be a little more hair-triggered and dangerous, but also possibly more readily confused and manipulated.

'Okay,' Parker said. 'I'm ready.'

11

Then the next problem was the vehicle. They'd come downstairs, Parker being careful to rub along the wall, not wanting to lose his balance without hands to protect him in a fall, and the guy said, 'My truck's a block from here. You just walk a little ahead of me.'

'You'll want to take my car,' Parker told him. 'It's about a block and a half that way.'

'Leave it, you can come back for it,' the guy said. 'We'll take my truck.'

'You want the car,' Parker insisted. He knew the guy was thinking about that shotgun in the truck, and wanted it with him, but Parker was thinking about the sixty-seven thousand dollars in the window well of the car.

The guy gave him an irritated look. 'What's your problem? You think the car's more comfortable, because you're cuffed? I don't care about that. We'll take the truck.'

'The point is,' Parker told him, 'when we drive in there, if we're in the car, they won't shoot us.'

The guy frowned at him, trying to work out if that was true.

Parker said, 'We just pulled a major job last night, everybody's tense. We killed the guy owned that shack, we know the kind of people he hung out with. Some truck shows up, they won't think twice.'

'I don't know about this,' the guy said.

'Whatever you need out of the truck, get it and throw it in the car.' And all the time, he had to be careful to say 'truck' and not 'pickup,' because the guy hadn't called it a pickup and he wasn't supposed to know Parker had ever seen it.

Many things, though, were making him suspicious and antsy. He said, 'What do you mean, what I need out of the truck?'

'Suitcase, whatever you've got,' Parker explained. 'You aren't carrying anything *on* you.'

'What is this car?'

'Lexus. A block and a half that way. The keys are in my right side pocket here.'

'Keys.' The guy didn't even like that, having to come close enough to get hold of the keys.

Parker knew they both knew what he might try at that point; the lunge, the kick, get the guy down and use the feet on him, hoping to get at the key for the cuffs later. But Parker wouldn't do it that way; there was too much chance the .38 could go off, and nobody could know for sure where the bullet would go.

Nothing to do but wait. Words of reassurance would not reassure, they'd merely make him more spooked than ever. Parker stood there, patient, and the guy slowly worked it through, and then he said, 'Face to the wall. Put your forehead on the wall. Don't move anything.' Absolutely a cop.

Again the cool gun barrel touched the back of his neck. The hand burrowed into his pocket like a small animal, and withdrew, and then the barrel also withdrew.

'All right.'

Parker turned around, and the guy had retreated to the middle of the living room. The keys to the Lexus were in his left hand, the .38 in his right. *'Now* we go,' he said. 'I'll open the front door and step to the side. You go out, I follow. You stay just ahead of me and we walk to your car.'

'A block and a half, in cuffs? What if somebody sees them?'

'Maybe I'm arresting you.'

'And what if the somebody's a patrol car? This is a middle-class neighborhood, no crime but a lot of voters. This is where the cops like to patrol.'

The guy started to sneer, as though about

to defend cops, but then must have realized how stupid that would be. Instead, he looked around, saw the shut closet door over near the front door, and went over to open it. He rummaged around and brought out a raincoat. 'You'll wear this,' he said. 'Over your shoulders. Stand still.'

Parker stood still. The guy brought the raincoat to him, draped it on his shoulders, and stepped back to consider him. 'Works fine,' he decided.

It probably did, though too short. 'Okay,' Parker said. 'Now what?'

'Now we walk,' the guy said, and opened the door.

The gray day was still gray, the neighborhood still mostly empty, people now off to their jobs or schools. Parker, with the guy to his left and one pace behind him, walked down the street, crossed to the other side after they'd passed where the pickup was parked over there, and stopped at the Lexus.

'Is it locked?'

'Of course.'

The guy unlocked it, and said, 'Get in.'

'Two things,' Parker said. 'Could you take this coat off me? Throw it in the back seat or on the ground or whatever you want. And just give me a hand on the elbow to help me in.'

'I'm your goddam nurse,' the guy said, and yanked the coat off him, and let it drop to the curb. 'Get in the car, I'll help if you need it.'

He needed it; balance was impossible, to shift from standing outside the car to sitting inside it. As he was about to topple, the guy grabbed his right elbow with his left hand, his right hand staying in his pocket with the .38. He pulled back, helped Parker get into position, seated there against his own arms pulled back behind him, and said, 'Don't move.' He reached across him to strap him in with the seat belt.

Parker said, 'Safety first?'

'*My* safety first,' the guy said. Then he shut the door, and went around to get behind the wheel.

Parker said, 'Where's your truck?'

'Don't worry about it.'

'I thought you wanted things from it.'

The guy started the engine. 'Where to?' he said.

12

The question was gasoline. It had been a while since the Lexus had been refueled. Parker had planned to do that after he finished with Cathman and got his day's sleep, and as he remembered, the last he'd looked at the gas gauge it had shown just under a quarter tank. It was hard to see that little arrow from this angle, in the passenger seat, and he didn't

268

want to be obvious about it.

He was trying now to go through the trips he'd taken with Mike Carlow, when they were looking for a place to stay, when they'd wound up at Tooler's cottages. Different real estate agents had shown them different things, driven them on different back roads. It was important now to remember them right, which road led where.

He needed a destination that would fit in with the story he'd told, in case they were still together that long. But it would be best if he could arrange the route so they arrived at the right kind of gas station when the needle was looking low. A small station, isolated, not too many customers, one guy on duty, no mechanics. So remember those places, too, and the different roads, and the different places the real estate agents had shown them.

Tiredness kept trying to creep in on him, distract him, but the discomfort of having his arms pulled around behind him, and then the weight of his torso against his arms, kept him from getting groggy. He thought about undoing the cuffs now, but he was afraid the freedom would make him careless, permit him to move his arms a little to relieve the pressure, and alert the guy beside him. So he left the cuffs where they were.

At first it was all major highways, across the Hudson River out of Albany and then due east toward Massachusetts. This was called the Thruway Extension and at the state line it would meet up with the Massachusetts Turnpike, one hundred fifty miles due east to Boston. A little before that, there was the north-south highway called the Taconic Parkway, the oldest major highway in the state, built in the twenties so the state government people in Albany would have easy access to New York City, one hundred fifty miles to the south and screw the rest of the state, which didn't get a big road until the thruway came in, thirty years later.

The Taconic was the road Parker and the others had been using between the Tooler cottages and Albany, but not today. Some miles before that turnoff was State Route 9, also north-south. 'We take that exit,' Parker said.

The guy was suspicious of everything. 'Isn't there a bigger road up ahead?'

'Out of our way, too far east,' Parker told him. 'We crossed the river, remember? Now we gotta go south, and then back west to the river. This is the turn.'

The guy frowned, but took it, and they drove southward through low hills covered with trees wearing their bright green new spring leaves, and here and there a little town with one intersection and a traffic light. And a gas station, usually, but not the kind Parker wanted.

Time to get off this road. 'You'll take the
270

next right,' he said. 'There's a dark brown church at the corner, little graveyard.'

But there wasn't; a different intersection appeared, with a farm stand on the corner, all its display shelves empty, not yet open for the season, nothing yet grown ripe enough to sell.

The guy pulled to a stop in front of the empty stand and said, 'All right, what's the story?' He was driving with the .38 tucked into his belt, just behind the buckle, and now his right hand rested on the butt.

'It must be the next one,' Parker said.

'Where we headed? Just tell me where we're going, and I'll go there.'

'I can't tell you that,' Parker said. 'This isn't my neighborhood, I just came here a few weeks ago to do the ship. I don't know the names of things and route numbers and all that, I just know how to get from one place to another. I forgot about this intersection, that's all, it'll be the next one.'

'If it isn't,' the guy said, 'we'll try a different idea.'

'Fine. It's the next one.'

The guy started the Lexus forward, and three miles farther on they came to the intersection with the old brown church. 'See?' Parker said. 'I'm not an old-time native here, that's all. But I know where I'm going. You take this right, and it comes to a T, and then you take the right off that.'

'The right? That sends me north again.'

'No, it doesn't,' Parker said. 'These roads twist all over the place, because of the hills, and because they laid out the farms before they laid out the roads. We won't go north any more, don't worry about it.'

But they would. The second right would send them north, to a different road that would send them west again, if they went that far. Parker was grateful for the cloud cover; if the sun was out, it would be a lot harder to move this guy around into the right position.

Before they reached the T, Parker glanced over at the dashboard to see the fuel-low warning light gleaming red. 'How long's that been on?'

The guy didn't look down from the twisty road. 'What?'

'Low on gas, the light's on.'

The guy gave it a quick look. 'We're all right,' he said. 'It isn't far now, is it?'

'In and back out? I don't know. How long's the light been on?'

'Not long,' the guy said, but out of irritation, not conviction.

'You're in charge,' Parker said, 'but if I was driving, and I come across a gas station, I'd put in a few bucks.'

'We're fine,' the guy said.

As they'd been driving, to ease the tendency to cramp in his shoulders and upper arms, Parker had been rolling his shoulders, exercising them from time to time, keeping

272

them limber. The guy hadn't liked it the first time he'd done it, but then he'd realized the reason, and hadn't minded after that. Now, as they approached that T, Parker rolled his shoulders, and this time he hunched his butt forward just a little on the seat, which increased the pain and pressure on his arms at the same time that it gave his hands some room between his body and the seat-back. The fingers of his left hand plucked the paperclip out of his right palm. Both hands worked at straightening one end of the clip. Then the fingers of his left hand found the lock in the middle of the cuffs and bent it up so that it gouged into his flesh, but the fingers of his right hand could insert the end of the clip, holding fast to the part that was still bent.

He'd done this before; it would be painful for a while now, but not impossible. He probed with the end of the clip, feeling the resistance, feeling where it gave. There.

'The T will be coming up in a couple minutes,' he said, the words covering the faint click, already muffled by the seat and his body, as the lock released on the right cuff.

That was enough. He could undo the left cuff later, and in the meantime it could be useful.

They reached the T, and turned right. Parker rolled his shoulders, clenched and released his hands. His arms stung as the blood moved sluggishly through them.

'We turn left up ahead,' he said. 'There's an intersection with a Getty station and a convenience store.'

'If it's there,' the guy said.

'No, it's there. I got the church off by one, but this is right. You see the sign? There it is.'

The red and white Getty gas station sign was the only thing out ahead of them that wasn't green. It was a small place, two pumps, a small modular plastic shop behind it that had been built in an afternoon. There were fishermen's landings nearby, and a few small manufacturing businesses tucked away discreetly in the hills, not to offend the weekenders with the sight of commerce, so there was enough business to keep this gas station open, but rarely was it busy.

It was empty now. The guy slowed for the intersection, and Parker kept quiet. Push him, and he'd push the other way. And if this place didn't work, there was one cabin that had been shown to them by one of the real estate agents that they hadn't liked because there was no easy way to get down to the river—you were supposed to admire the view, not enter it—but that would do very well now, if necessary. Be better if it hadn't been rented to anybody, but Parker would take what came.

'Maybe I will stop.'

Parker nodded, but didn't say anything. The guy angled in toward the pumps. 'I also gotta take a leak,' he said. Parker had been counting

274

on that. Almost always, people want to take a leak before they go into something dangerous or intensive or important to them. This guy didn't want to face five armed people that he meant to rob, and be thinking about his bladder.

'I could do the same,' Parker said.

'You can wait,' the guy told him. 'Encourage you to get us there quicker.' He pulled his shirttail out, so it would cover the gun in his belt, and climbed out of the Lexus, shutting the door.

Parker sat facing front while the guy pumped gas, and then watched to see if he'd pay first or go to the men's room first, and he headed around the side to the men's room.

The second he was out of sight, Parker unhooked the seat belt and got out of the car. The cuffs dangled from his left wrist. He put his fingers through the right cuff, and held it like brass knuckles, as he strode across the asphalt and around to the side of the building, where the two doors stood side by side, MEN and WOMEN, with a broad concrete step in front of both.

Scrubland back here led to woods and nothing else. There was no one around. Parker stood to the left of the door marked MEN, facing the building, left arm cocked at his chest. He held the ballpoint pen in his right fist, gripped for stabbing. He waited, and the doorknob made a noisy turn, and the door

275

opened outward, and as the guy appeared, in profile, Parker drove the metaled left fist across his chest on a line directly into that bandaged ear.

The guy screamed. He threw both hands up, and Parker stabbed for his right eye with the pen, but one of the guy's flailing arms deflected it, and the pen sank into his cheek instead, high up, through the flesh, then scraping leftward over teeth and gums.

The guy was trying to shout something, but Parker was too busy to listen. His left fist, inside the handcuff, chopped at the cheek and the pen jutting out of it while his right hand reached inside the shirt and yanked out the .38.

The guy staggered backward, wide-eyed, blood running down from under the bandage covering that ear, more blood running down his cheek, spilling out of his mouth. He slammed into the sink behind him, but he was scrabbling for his left hip pocket, so that's where Parker's Python would be.

Parker stepped into the room, pulling the door shut behind himself. The guy's hand was in that pocket, closing around something, when Parker shot him just above the belt buckle.

The bullet went through the guy and cracked the sink behind him, and he sagged back, staring, just beginning to feel the shock. Parker stepped forward, shifting the .38 to his left hand where the cuffs dangled downward again, blood-streaked now, while he reached around and got the Python out of the left hip pocket. Then he put the Python away, because it would be much louder than the .38, switched the .38 to his right hand, and then collected from another pocket Cathman's four-page dream. He stashed that inside his shirt, then reached around the guy to find and collect his wallet. Then he stepped back, .38 in right hand, wallet in left, and the guy folded both hands over his stomach where the bullet had gone in. He stared at Parker with dulled and unbelieving eyes.

'Now,' Parker said, 'we can talk.'

13

The guy said, 'I'm . . . I'm gut-shot,' as though it should be a surprise to Parker, too.

Parker opened the wallet one-handed, looked at the ID in there, looked up. 'Raymond Becker,' he said. 'You're a cop, Ray? I thought you might be a cop.'

'I need an ambulance, man.'

'Local cop, far from home. Sit down on the toilet there,' Parker advised him. 'Keep holding it in, you'll be all right.'

'I'm gonna die! I need an ambulance.'

Parker said, 'I could shoot off your other

ear, just to attract your attention. Or you could concentrate. Sit down there.'

Ray Becker concentrated. His breathing came loud and ragged, bouncing off the tile walls. He looked at Parker, and saw no help. Slowly, both hands pressed to his bleeding gut, he slid along the cracked sink to his right, and dropped backward with a little bark of pain on to the closed toilet lid.

Meanwhile, Parker studied Becker's ID some more. 'You don't act like most cops, Ray,' he said. 'Particularly far from home. You act more like a guy on the run, desperate for a stake.'

'I played my hand,' Becker said. He sounded weaker. 'I lost. But I don't have to *die.*' He was clenching his teeth now, pushing the words through them. The sweat drops that had started to form on his brow, silvery hobnails in the glare of the overhead light, reminded Parker of Marshall Howell.

He said the name aloud: 'Marshall Howell.'

The name seemed to sink slowly into Becker's consciousness, like a bone dropped into a lake. Parker watched him, and saw his eyes gradually focus, saw him at last look at Parker with a new kind of fear.

Parker nodded. He waved the wallet. 'I see where you're from, Ray.'

Becker said, *'You*—were the other one—in the car?'

'And walked off with the money, Ray. You

278

were a little quicker, we could've met then.'

Becker blinked, but he didn't have anything to say.

'You didn't have a lot of time,' Parker told him. 'I guess you were already in trouble, you look like that kind. He wouldn't give you me, but he gave you Cathman, and here you come, on the run, gonna kill the whole world if you have to, get your hands on fuck-you money.'

'He was dying anyway,' Becker said.

'He was not,' Parker told him. 'But he should have been. I knew it was a mistake to let him live.'

He put the .38 an inch from Ray Becker's left eye. Becker was saying all kinds of things, panting and spitting out words. 'We live and learn, Ray,' Parker said, and shot him.

14

Inside the cramped and crowded convenience store was one person, the kid seated on the stool in the narrow space behind the cash register, reading a paperback book. A small black plastic portable radio, dangling by its handle from a hook on the wall above and behind the kid's head, played tinny rock music, pretty loud; another reason he hadn't heard the two shots in the men's room, at the far end of the building. Which was good, it meant he

279

wasn't another problem to be dealt with.

Parker had come around to the store directly from finishing with Becker because he wanted to know if the clerk in here had heard anything and was about to raise an alarm, but the answer was no. So the thing to do was pay the ten dollars out of Becker's wallet for the gas Becker had pumped, meaning the kid still had no reason to remember him or even notice him, and then drive away.

He told himself he should find a motel soon, he was weary and sore, it was almost nine o'clock in the morning, but the adrenaline still pumped through him after Becker, and his exhaustion was offset by nervous tension. He'd left the .38 with Becker, along with the handcuffs, and now the Python was stashed inside the back seat of the Lexus. As he drove, he shredded Cathman's confession, dropping scraps of it out the window for miles.

He stopped the littering as he passed the road in to Tooler's cottages, where a patrol car was parked along the verge and a bored cop walked around on the dirt road, there to keep the curious and the press and the mistaken away from the scene of murder and arson within.

A few miles later, the Lexus crested a hill, and off to the right he could see the river, looking sluggish and dark under the gray sky. At first it was just the river, mottled, slate gray, but then a sailboat appeared out there, a white triangle of sail.

The Lexus drove down the other side of the hill.